SCRIB

SCRIB

Some Characters, Adventures,
Letters and Conversations from the Year 1863,
Including a Deadly Chase
In the Wilderness of the Fearsome Canyon,
All as Told by Billy Christmas,
Who Was There

a novel by

DAVID IVES

 HarperCollins*Publishers*

For information address HarperCollins Publishers,
1350 Avenue of the Americas,
New York, NY 10019.
www.harperchildrens.com
Library of Congress Cataloging-in-Publication Data
Ives, David.
Scrib : a novel / by David Ives.— 1st ed.
p. cm.
Summary: In 1863, a sixteen-year-old boy nicknamed Scrib travels around the
West making his living writing and delivering letters, an occupation that leads to
him nearly getting killed, being jailed as a criminal, joining up with the notorious
Crazy James Kincaid, and delivering a letter from President Abraham Lincoln to a
Paiute Indian.
ISBN 0-06-059841-7 — ISBN 0-06-059842-5 (lib. bdg.)
[1. Adventure and adventurers—Fiction. 2. West (U.S.)—History—Civil War,
1861–1865—Fiction. 3. Letter writing—Fiction.] I. Title.
PZ7.I948Sc 2005
[Fic]—dc22   2004012483
Typography by Larissa Lawrynenko
1 2 3 4 5 6 7 8 9 10
❖
First Edition

This book is dedicated
With gratitude and affection
To James Chace,
Who spent his youth on Treasure Island
With the Count of Monte Cristo,
And who taught me letters

CONTENTS

So he looked not behind him, but fled
towards the middle of the plain . . . till he
came at the House of the Interpreter,
where he knocked, over and over; at last
someone came to the door, and asked
who was there.

JOHN BUNYAN
The Pilgrim's Progress

SCRIB

IN WHICH I FIND MY SELF PURSUED

Middle of a morning, I rode down out the pines
and come into the scrub. At the place on the
grade where the pines left off and the scrub took
over, I stopped and loosed the reins so Gabe
could get at some of the last sweet grass along the crick.
Then I sat a while and looked over the country I was
coming into and pondered it somewhat troubledly. It was
the old scrub down there all right. I could see some fine
country far beyond it, very small and green, and to the
north I could feel the great Canyon even though I couldn't
see it—same way I always knew the War betwixt
Unions and Confederates was going on somewhere
though I had not been to it. Ever minute or two Gabe

kept looking back up towards the ridge and stamping his left forehoof, and I would stroke his neck to try and calm him. Problem was, I didn't feel any too calm myself.

Somebody was following me. I knew so because I had read my pursuer's fearful message.

Afternoon before, I had found a fine camp up among the pinion pines and junipers just down from the ridge. I have always liked to be among pines, for the resiny smell and the soft gold blanket of needles they throw on the ground and for the homey feeling you get when the light shines through the spaces betwixt them. In the spot that I found, a spring bubbled up out of nowhere and run away down the hill in a crick. It was fringed by mallow and horsetail, and that crick had the sweetest water I ever tasted. After I had et, I scrubbed my tins clean with horsetail, which is a trick I learnt from my Paiute customer, Pierre.

So I was feeling pretty carefree reposing there, whistling and tossing bits of wood on the fire, counting the stars as they popped out like zeroes on the end of some long number. Then I heard Gabe snuffle amongst the trees where I had tied him and I stopped whistling, fast. When I saw Gabe dance around so he could look up into the dark of the ridge and he posed the tip of that left forehoof on the ground like a pointer dog, I slid up to my feet and eased my knife out of its sheath.

"What do you see up there, Gabe?" I whispered.

Gabe couldn't see any more than me in that darkness, but he could smell something, or sense it. That's why his ears was laid back and his nostrils was big and his hoof was posed. That left forehoof was always a telltale, and it didn't look like Gabe had smellt bear or bobcat. He had sensed something very bad up there, which could only mean Man.

My rifle was a long jump away, but a boy of sixteen with a rusty squirrel rifle wasn't going to be much good in a real fight—specially if that rifle wasn't loaded and the boy had swore to his mother never to fire a weapon at another human being. I tossed a few more chunks on the fire and banged my tins to scat the thing away, but nothing scatted up there that I heard.

"Hello!" I called out, but my voice didn't come out too loud so I tried again. "Hello, there! If you're after food," I called, "I still got some salt pork, and you're welcome to it!"

All I heard was the tree toads and the fire crackle and the rustle of the stream. I had just convinced my self it was nothing but a ringtail cat when I heard the sound.

Tching. Like a boot spur ringing on a rock somewheres up there. And just a hair too quickly muted.

3

A breeze come up and fanned the flames, but the greater brightness around me only made the dark look darker. Anybody up there could have seen me edging towards that rifle, still keeping my knife at the ready. Not that I would have known what to do with the knife. I wasn't a rough-in-tumble kid, and I only weight a hunderd twenty with my hair unbarbered.

"If you want anything," I called, "I ain't got it! I ain't got nothin' a-tall! I'm just a poverished boy!"

A rancher had been robbed and brutely clubbed to death two weeks before, and Wanted posters was up all over the landscape with the face of Crazy James Kincaid offering $5000.00 reward. I hoped I wasn't about to find the Kincaid Gang without planning to. And the "Crazy" on "Crazy James Kincaid" had not been added for decoration. People said Kincaid had once shot a man for telling a joke he did not find funny.

I finally made it to my rifle, but loading it took some time what with my shaking hands. The ramrod in the muzzle clanged like a church bell. When I finally got the thing fired up, I stood there listening, wondering if I was just spooked and regretting my lively imagination.

"Go home!" I shouted into the dark. "Go on home!"

But still nothing scatted away.

That was not the first time in my life I kept a big fire

going all night, but it was the first time I ever slept with my rifle. There must be a trick to sleeping with a firearm, for a couple times I rolled over and practicly blew my own head off. By the time a moon slid up as bright as a new dime, I was exhausted from waiting for it. I tried lullabying myself to sleep with "The Lord is my Shepherd, I shall not want," and it worked, too, but ever so often a mouse'd skitter by and I'd start awake in a sweat before I remembered what the sweat was for.

Suddenly it was daylight and the fire was out and that shiny-dime moon had thinned out as sere as onionskin.

"Good moonin', moon," I said, for no reason but to hear my own voice. I liked the sound of my voice so much I reutterated that and sung it and proclaimed it to my own amusement while I boiled coffee and packed up camp. For anybody watching I looked awful calm, cept my tin cup rattled against my teeth and I spillt coffee all down my front. That had seemed such a good camp, what with the sweet crick and the pines and all. Well, nothing keeps anyway.

Being alone too much you can fall prey to tricks, and I had been tricking my self ever since I rose that day. For in all the time I was breakfasting, I had never once looked up towards the ridge. There could have been a great green elephant standing ten foot upwards of me and I would not have known it. So as I was tying my blanket behind the saddle, I stopped and took a breath.

You gotta look, Scrib, I said to myself, *for your own self's sake. Mazewell know thy enemy.*

So I looked up towards the ridge and saw nothing and nobody there, just the pines and a crop of white boulders farther up the top. I had my boots on, I was saddled up and packed, I could have rode away right then and there. But I knew my own tricks.

Go on up, Scrib, I thought to myself. *Mazewell have a thoro look.*

Gabe kept a eye on me as I scooched up the pines towards the ridge. I didn't take the rifle with me, as I perferred to believe everthing was just fine. I didn't want to put myself into a fool state again anyway.

Then I found some signs.

Fifty yards up from where I had camped was those white boulders, and the needles behind the boulders was all scuffed away where somebody had stood a long while. The dirt on the boulders was brushed away where the person had lent his elbows, and black tobacco bits was mixed in the needle scuff where the person had smoked a cigar. I followed the scuff marks up to the ridge and I scanned the slope below a long time, but nothing stirred down there. Then I went back down to the white boulders and pondered.

That was when I saw my enemy's message.

I didn't know it was a message at first. I thought it was where the person had scraped his cigar out on those boulders. But the scrape looked too regular, and I saw that the tar-black ash made letters on the flat stone, spelling something out.

D I E

My heart jumped up my throat at that, and pounded in my ears. I wanted to protest. I wanted to say, I didn't do it, whatever it was. I wanted to say they had the wrong boy, only I didn't have anybody to say it to. Instead, I bruptly chucked up my breakfast on the pine needles at my feet. I have never been much of a one for danger.

That done, I won't say I kept my dignity. I skittered back down the slope so fast I splashed right through the crick up to my ankles and run on fifty feet too far. In half a trice I was up on Gabe and we was gone, riding down the grade alongside the stream.

We descended with me facing backwards most of the way, imagening all manner of ambushes. Where the pines ended and the scrub was about to start, I let Gabe

7

taste the sweet grass by the crick one more time whilst I had that ponder. All down the slope below me, ocotillo plants sprung up out the ground like long green skeleton fingers groping from the sand. The slope was so still I heard the *whoop, whoop, whoop* of its wings as a raven flew by me, and I seemed to see its every black wing feather. As a omin, it mazewell have been a coal-black cat flying cross my path.

I wondered was it safer to ride in the open of the scrub or hide in the shadows of the pines? And why had someone picked me to pursue, a boy with nothing to his name but letters? I don't know how long I sat my saddle pondering, when a Preacher rises up like a pillar of darkness from the foot of an ocotillo down the slope and shakes his fist at me. I had the fear of God in me already, so I startled.

"What in tarnation are you doin' sittin' there, boy?" he cries out, and I wondered if I had suprized him in the midst of some personal toiletry. "There ain't nothin' here," he cries, and points a hand downwards. "Move on, boy! Move on!"

"I beg your pardon, Preacher," I called out, and he says, "Don't you beg my pardon! Heaven's a-callin' and she lies that-away!"

He kept waving me downwards into the scrub, and I

figgered, mazewell go now as ever, so I moved on. The Preacher watched me go, all the time I went.

A hunderd yards down the slope, the sweet water thinned out and bubbled down into the ground and the crick puddled and disappeared on the sand like it had never been, just as mysterious as it had come into being. I wondered if the crick bubbled out someplace else or did the waters descend into the middle of the earth never to be heard from again. Any case, for fear of quicksand I rode round the soft ground that had sucked up the crick and picked up my pace, for I had my circuit to make. I figgered business would take my mind off things.

A scorpion flicked its tail out from under a stone, and I descended into the scrub.

Chapter Two

ATTACK AT THE TRIPLE X RANCH

omulus Vollmer called his place the Triple X Ranch, and it was probly the sorriest spread of desert this side of Mungolia. Queer thing was, you could not feel sorry for Romulus Vollmer. He was so blissful being the perprietor of the Triple X Ranch you got kinda excited on his behalf. He was on his own, with a hunderd head of skelety cattle, and he didn't need a thing to make his life complete cept his sweetheart, Jenny Smeed. Rom greeted me out front of what he called his hacienda, which was a shack of about twelve by twelve, and tottery as a stack of mis-match dishes. I always had a special feeling for Rom, as he was my first customer when I come to the Hill City district two years before.

"Come on in, Scrib," he says in rubber boots up to his armpits. "We got love letters to write."

I got Gabe settled in the stable and unstrapped my work bag. Whilst I was slipping the bag over my shoulder, something on a far hill caught the side of my eye—a glint, or a flash, or a flicker of light on metal. Whatever it was, it was gone before I turned to look and didn't come again. I wondered if somebody was up there—maybe somebody who smoked a couple tar-black cigars above my camp last night.

"Love letters, Scrib!" Romulus called to me from inside.

The inside of Romulus's "hacienda" matched its outside like a cut-rate Bible and its paper cover. There was a bare plank floor with a stove and a table and two chairs, a cot with a shotgun and a fiddle hanging over it, and a photograph of Jenny Smeed nailed up on the wall. The photo sure did not flatter her beauty. In true life Jenny was a fetching girl who swelled plentifully in all the right places, but in the picture she looked like a ham with two beady eyes wearing a frilly dress and its hands folded. The way Romulus revered that picture, I wondered if his eyes was faulty.

Romulus says, "You got a letter from Jenny?"

"I sure do," I said.

Romulus slid into a chair by the table, pointed me into the other one, and turned up the lantern wick.

"I'm ready," he said. "Unstick and read."

Truth is, I would have perferred a wash-up and some food. I could smell stew and collyflowers from the pots on the stove. Romulus liked collyflowers, I think because the word had the word "flower" in it. I my self dislike collyflowers because they live on inside the body as air, and in a twelve-by-twelve hacienda things can get stinky pretty fast with two males stuffed fulla collyflowers. Anyway, much as I would have liked some victules, this was my job and I had to do it, hungry or un.

I took Jenny's letter out my writing bag. Like usual, she had chose the delooks 3-cent pink stationery with the tea roses and matching envelope. Now, in my experience, folks differ on the opening of envelopes same as they differ on stationeries. For a sealed envelope is like a closed door. Your whole life might be different for better or worse once you step through it and find out what's on the other side. So some folks perfer you to open their letters for them, while others like to unstick their letters them selves. Some folks poke their finger under the flap and tear the thing open like they're gutting a fish. Some slit it cleanly with a blade. Others unpaste the flap real careful to keep the envelope neat for their personal rememberabilia. Just like with everthing, people are various.

Romulus perferred me to do the honors, and I give him my full un-sticking fanfare. First I dusted my hands on my trousers, then unsheathed my knife and took about ten minutes working it under the flap so's not to damage it. Rom sat there mezmerized through the whole ceremony. Then I cleared my throat and blew my nose and folded and stowed my handkerchief very solicitrously. Finally I worked the letter out like it was made of wafer and might crumble into dust.

"That envelope," Romulus said with wonder, "contains air from inside the house of Jenny Smeed!"

"Yes, sir," I said. "I guess it does."

"Air that Jenny herself has breathed."

"Yes, sir," I said.

"Let me breathe in that letter," he said.

I passed the envelope to Romulus and he stuck his nose inside it and inhaled till his eyes was dopey.

"Go on and read," he said, and settled himself to listen. I leant forward into the lantern glow and read.

"'May 23, 1863,'" I started. "'My dearest and most precious sweetest darling Romulus, How are you. I am fine but my Elbow hurts.'"

"Her elbow hurts?" Romulus said. "Why? What's the matter?"

"Maybe she'll explain it," I said, like I didn't know already. I had writ the letter and it was in my handwriting, a course.

"Maybe she will," he said. "Read on, Scrib."

"'I am fine but my Elbow hurts, because I burnt it on the stove pipe but I smeared some butter on it. Now it's fine.'"

"Did her elbow look fine?" Rom said.

"It looked fine to me," I said.

"I'd take care of her elbow all right," he said. "I'd smear a whole tub of butter on it. And she's got real pretty elbows, Scrib," he said. "With two dimples right here." He pointed on his sleeve.

"I have seen the dimples, Rom."

"Are those dimples something?" he said.

I said, "Her elbow dimples are awe-enspiring."

"And the dimples is the least of her," he said. "Jenny Smeed is a full-uptuous woman."

For a man who had only seen Jenny half a dozen times all told, Romulus sure knew her accouterments in detail. The two of them had enjoyed what Romulus called a world-wind romance. He proposed and she accepted, but Jenny's father said they had to separate and wait a full year to see whether the Romance gelled or puddled out. If Jenny's mother had been alive, I doubt things would have gone that way. Jenny's mother was the kind would have said, "You love each other? Then hold out your fingers and put rings on them. The proof is in the putting."

"Keep readin', Scrib," Rom said.

"'The chickens are laying with a real fury . . .'"

"Good," he nodded.

"'. . . and Cobb has built us a new outhouse . . .'"

"Excellent," he said. "Outhouses is vital."

"'. . . complete with that new toilet seat from Abilene.'"

"Wonderful," he said. "Wonderful."

"'O my Soul mate,' she now writes."

Rom let out a yelp and drummed on the table.

"Here comes the good part," he cried. "Read it nice and slow."

I cleared my throat.

"'O my Soul mate, behold! Long and dark and woesome are the slatey-black nights without thy person nigh to me. How I miss thee forsooth.'"

"For who?" he said.

"Forsooth," I said.

He said, "What's a sooth?"

"'Forsooth' is poetry," I said. "It kinda means . . . well it means 'forsooth.' Same way 'indeed' means 'indeed.'"

"I like it indeed," he said. "Read on, forsooth."

"'Woe is me, fond lover, for I languish from woe without thee. Fain would I see thee ere morning.'"

"'Fain,'" said Romulus. "Is that another word for 'forsooth'?"

"'Fain' means 'I wish.'"

"Then I fain you to read on."

"'The fates have decreed we must be sundered, but eftsoons we will meet again. Dearest heart I implant a thousand kisses on thee from the bottomless depths of my bosoms. Your Humble and Obedient Servant, Jennifer B. Smeed.'"

What Jenny had actually to me said was, "Tell him I miss him, Scrib, ever night and ever day. Tell him I wish he was here right now. And tell him I kiss him from far away over and over again. I miss him, and I kiss him."

I had translated all that into love-letter lingo, which is one of my free extra services. Jenny had been unnormally worked up during this pertickler letter, and cried time and again as we sat writing it, drying her eyes on her apron. I didn't see how she was going to wait a whole year for him, weeping at that rate.

When I had done reading, Romulus sighed like a

man who had just et a steak. "That's real pretty," he said. "But how come she signs it 'Your Humble and Obedient Servant,' stead of 'XXX Love,' like usual?"

"All the best letter writers are using 'Your Humble and Obedient Servant' these days," I said. "Salesmen. Lawyers. Undertakers."

"Would you fain eat now, Scrib?" he said.

"Forsooth I would," I said.

"I'll dish the grub while you wash up."

The sun was set when I went outside, with just a low band of orange light topping the distance like sherbet. The evening air felt refreshful, so after I washed my hands and bathed my face and the back of my neck, I stood at the pump cooling off, listening to some coyotes complaining somewhere in coyote language. My Injun friend Pierre would know what they was saying, what with all his Paiute wisdom.

Then I heard a *tching!* from out the darkness and I forgot all about coyotes. It sounded like the same spur as last night, and the person wearing it wasn't all that far away. I didn't wait for inlightenment. I scuttled back inside the hacienda before that spur could get any closer, and latched the door.

Romulus was throwing pots and plates around in such a love lather, he didn't notice. I didn't tell him what

I had heard out there, or what I had seen writ in ashes on that boulder up the ridge. I guess I foolishly believed if somebody was looking for me, it was my own problem.

Rom twirled two platefuls of stew and collyflowers onto the table before me. I convinced myself I had been hearing things, and we had us two a jolly dinner. We "forsooth'd" and "fain'd" a lot. We even "eftsoon'd" a time or two. When I did remember that sound in the dark and Romulus asked if I was troubled, I blamed it on collyflower gas. For we two sure was stinking up his hacienda.

After supper I spread out my choice of stationeries. Like usual, Romulus picked the pale blue paper for 4 cents and a matching 2-cent envelope. While I got out my pens and nibs and ink bottle, he took down the fiddle and scraped out "Pig Town Fling" and a couple choruses of "Beulah Land."

"I'm ready," I said, with the pen poised over the page like his bow over the fiddle.

"'Dear Jenny,'" he said. "How should we say that, Scrib?"

"Howbout," I said, "'Most precious mistress of the moon and stars of Heaven.'"

"I like it," he said. "Nice and direct."

Tching.

I said, "Did you hear something outside, Rom?"

I was sure I had heard that spur again, this time just outside the door, as if somebody had his ear to it listning.

"Why?" Rom said. "You expecting somebody?" He laughed, and I attempted to. Then he stopped and scratched his chin. "Now I think about it, there *was* somebody here looking for you."

"Looking for me?" I said.

"Colored fella," Rom said. "Said he was looking for a William Christmas. I said I didn't know anybody by that name, then I membered that was you."

"That's me," I said. "A colored fella, you say?"

"Large man," he said. "Beat-up face and a black hat with a blue band around her."

"What did you tell him?" I said.

"I said you wasn't too hard to find," Rom said, "always doing your circuit. I said you was bound to come by here sometime."

"Then what," I said.

"Then nothing," Rom said. "He thanked me and he got up on his hoss and took off."

I said, "Did he smoke a tar-black cigar?"

"I don't recollect," Rom said. "He wasn't here but five minutes."

"When did all this happen?" I said, and he said, "Maybe a week or two gone by."

Tching.

"Did you hear something just then?" I said.

Rom said, "You sure are jumpy tonight, Scrib."

I gave Romulus a good four bits' worth of letter that evening, but my mind was not on it. I was always half listning for that *tching* outside the door and wondering about this colored fella looking for me. I thought of Crazy James Kincaid out there on the loose and that rancher up towards Sullivan who got clubbed to death.

"Scrib," Rom said while I was stowing my writing tools, "Scrib, do you think I should go off to this War?"

"Why?" I said. "For Jenny's sake?"

"No," he said, "for the sake of . . . I don't know," he said. "For the War's sake. For the Union."

"That War is in the states," I said. "I'm not part of any Union out here. I got no dog in that fight."

"Maybe—," Rom was saying, when suddenly something went *whang* against the cabin door and some glass shattered and there was a explosion.

"What the Jesus was that?" Romulus said, and then the whole door bust into a roaring sheet of flame. Somebody outside had throwd the stable lantern at the door and set us afire.

"Let's go," said Rom, and headed for the door to kick through it, for that door was the only way out.

I grabbed his arm.

"Hold it, Rom," I said. "Take your gun."

"My gun?" he said. "Why?" We was already having to raise our voices over the crackling roar.

"Somebody's out there after me, and I bet he's waiting for me to come out."

Rom looked into my eyes and took it all in at once. He unhooked the shotgun over the cot, then he took the photo of Jenny off the wall and stuffed her in his shirt pocket and grabbed a box of shells. I took my writing bag, for that was precious. The cabin was getting very hot and smoky, but if we went busting through that flaming door we was gonna be ambushed blind. Half the wall was ablaze already. We'd bake alive if we didn't get out real fast.

"Let's go the back way," he said.

"The what?" I said.

He threw the cot aside and revealed a low trap in the wall behind it.

"I might be simple," he said, "but I ain't stupid."

He unhooked the trap and threw it open, and the breeze that blew in fanned up the wall of fire like a bellows.

"Go on," he shouted, and I rolled through the trap into the night, and Rom slid out after me. Whoever had arsoned the cabin was screened from us by the sparks and smoke and flames. Keeping low, we stumbled towards the darkness a dozen steps away from the cabin. When we reached it, Rom touched my arm and nodded his head towards the stable, and we loped off that way. Just as we reached the stable, a shot rung out and chucked into the stable wall. We had been spotted.

Rom stuck his head round the wall for one second to scout a look, and pulled it back as another shot rung out and blew some splinters off the corner.

"Did you see him?" I said.

"Nope," he said. "Nothin'." He nodded for me to get inside the stable, and I did so, followed by him.

"Saddle up," he whispered. In the dark we saddled our horses as fast as anybody ever did. Rom kept his eye and his shotgun fixed on the stable door the whole while, for he'd have a clear shot at anybody trying to get in, with us in the dark and the other person in the light of the flames. Problem was, we'd be spiked square in that light the minute we rode out the stable.

"I'm sorry, Rom," I said. "I'm really sorry."

"It wasn't you," Rom said. He shook my hand. "Just give Jenny my letter and tell her I love her, Scrib."

Beyond the stable door lay the flicker-field of light thrown from the fire, and beyond that the darkness of the scrub.

"Keep your head down," Rom said, "and ride out fast and straight. Let's go!"

We give our horses the heel and bent low and raced each other for the door. The second we hit that light, Rom let off a blast into the darkness. Then somebody fired at us from our left, and a bullet whirred like a hummingbird right past my nose. I veered Gabe hard to the right, and as I went I saw Rom sitting backwards in his saddle, blasting orange sparks out the other barrel as he disappeared into the dark. Then I heard more gunshots. Then I heard nothing.

It took me probly two seconds to reach full darkness myself, but I rode and rode and rode without looking behind me again till I must have been half a mile away. Rom's hacienda flamed like a lamp in the middle of blackness.

I had fled my own home three years before; now I had been forced to flee another. I didn't know if Romulus got away all right. I didn't know who was out there wanting me to die and setting the world afire to get me. I didn't know anything. Using the burning house behind me as my compass needle, I rode away into the night.

Chapter Three

WHAT I HAD FLED

"**M**Y FATHR WAS A SEE-CAPTIN."
I was born William Stanley Christmas in Phila-
delphia Pennsylvania, which I scarcely remember,
for we left it when I was three. I must have been
five years old when I wrote those words about my sea-
captain father in big square letters on a paper with
straight lines drawn in. My mother, who had ruled in the
guide-lines for me, liked that first page of mine so much
she kept it in the drawer with her lavender sachet.
Lavender was my mother's color and scent. "Lavender
transforms a room, William," she liked to say, and she
sure lavendered our house up with avengence.

"Always remember you come of good family,

William," my mother would say about ever two or three minutes. "Your father was John Stanley Christmas, the captain of the *Arcadia*, flagship of the Arcadia line."

If we was sitting in the parlor, she would take a gold-framed daggertype of my father from amongst the brickle-brack on the mantel. I would be sitting on the carpet at her feet.

"This is *he*," she'd say. Never "him," like regular folks. "This is *he*."

The heavy frame looked bulky in her long pale piano-player fingers, but she didn't like me to touch it or hold it, only to look. The picture showed a dark-browed, muscular man with a cookieduster moustache. The kind of man you would trust but never want to cross.

"That is your father," she'd say, "and this is the *Arcadia*."

She'd set my father back on the mantel and take down a framed engraving of a great ship on the waves, fixed in frozen black waves like a toy boat stuck in cake icing. Below the picture was a line of printing that said, "The *Arcadia*, flagship of the Arcadia line." Mother would make me spell out A-R-C-A-D-I-A evertime, which was how I learnt letters so young.

"Don't fidgit, William."

"I ain't fidgiting," I'd say.

"*Am not* fidgiting," she'd say. And I'd fidgit just to vex her.

Here my mother would take a clipping from out the family Bible, a newspaper article that said, "Tragedy At Sea. *Arcadia* Sinks Off Brazil. All Lives Lost." Upon which she mediately got nostalgiac.

"I was sundered from my spouse," she would sigh, "and you at three years old lost your father to the heartless sea. I could not bear to look at the heartless sea anymore, so I accepted a post here in Saint Louis Missouri where the sea is a thousand miles away. Sit still, William."

I always bridled at being told to sit still. But I bridled about lots of things in Saint Louis Missouri. I bridled at going to a school where my mother was the one and only teacher. I bridled at how she tended to find a moral parabull in everthing, as if life was some kinda Sunday sermon. I bridled at her always correcting my grammer, since what's the use of grammer if you have to treat it like a prize chicken? I bridled at the cravat she made me wear everplace. I bridled at looking out our windows and seeing a white picket fence and regular rows of other houses with white picket fences. My father didn't look off his boat and see white picket fences—he saw the heartless sea, which might be heartless but at least she wasn't regular.

Most of all I bridled at learning letters. Mother had been reading me *The Pilgrim's Progress* and the pickarisk adventures of Don Key Haughty from the time I was in the cradle, and she named me after William Shakespeare, so I probly got ruint right there at birth. Ever two minutes she'd be telling me, "William, you could be a *brilliant* scholar if you did not have such imagenative spelling and grammer—though I will admit you write with a fine clear hand." How often I thought of Bunyan's Pilgrim stopping up his ears with his fingers against the pleases of his family and running in a circle crying out "Life, life, eternal life." I didn't know a thing about eternity, but I sure knew what it was like to call out for life.

Nor did I care for the quality of saints in *Saint* Louis Missouri. There was a night when I sat at the table in my room doing my syphers when I heard a commotion outside, coming from the river. Then out my window I see a mass of torches and lanterns and a crowd of people, with the men and boys whooping and shouting—but whooping for blood and not for joy. Round that time, Saint Louis was hung with posters and handbills saying LOST SLAVE, or RUNAWAY SLAVE SOUGHT, or HAVE YOU SEEN THIS SLAVE? The post office had a whole wall of notices like that, the faces of runaway slaves fluttering like dead leafs on a oak tree. This crowd outside now had caught one.

The slave was at the center of the mob, tethered by four ropes like a unruly horse. He must have been hiding in the river reeds when they found him, for his clothes was dripping and his legs muddy. Blood gushed out the side of his head, and his nose was broke where somebody had clubbed him cross the face. His eyes in the torchlight glowed red and terrible. I think he feared they was gonna hang him. Evertime he stumbled, the women in the crowd jeered and pelted him with clods of dirt.

As I watched, he veered and stumbled up against the stakes of our white picket fence. He looked up and saw me watching through my window, and for that one moment I was looking straight into that man's wide eyes and did not know what to do. A man took a whip to the slave's back and lashed him and the men tugged their ropes, and now my mother flew out the house in her nightdress, crying out, "Shame! Shame! Shame to you slavedrivers!" But though she continued to cry that, the slave got dragged by and the crowd passed out of sight. I never did finish my syphers that night. All I could see was that man's terrible eyes staring into mine.

Soon all my bridling and fidgiting turned into open warfare betwixt my mother and me. My manhood come upon me and I started shaving—least, once or twice I shaved a coupla dark hairs off my upper lip. Who knows, maybe too much lavender makes a man go mad, like jimsonweed. Anyway, the night before my thirteenth birthday I slippt out my bedroom window after prayers, took Gabe from out the stable, and never looked back. I left a envelope behind me on the kitchen table.

Dear Mother,

I am gone into the World, and will not come back. Please Do Not come east trying to find me as you never will. I stole 4 Dollars from your dror. I Will send them back, when I have them. God Bless You for All you have done for me.

Your Loving son William Stanley Christmas

It was sly of me, saying "Do Not come east trying to find me." She would never find me there because I wasn't going east a-tall. I was headed west. Had not my father run away to sea? And did not Bunyan's Pilgrim run away across the field crying out for life? If anybody was to blame, I figgered, it was my mother herself driving me.

Problem was, I knew what I was fleeing from but not what I was looking for. Nor did I know how I was to earn my bread in the great wide World. Then, not two days later, I had my calling handed to me. I was in a general store with my feet up on a barrel drinking my first sarsparilla as a free man, when I overhear two farmers talking at the counter.

"Now that my farm's all set up," says the one, "I want to fetch my brother out here, but I gotta get a letter to him."

"You can write, Eben," says the other.

"I can write all right," says Eben, "but nobody could read what I wrote."

"Joe'll write a letter for you," says the first, nodding to Joe, the owner of the store.

"Too busy," says Eben.

"Wade Stewart'll do it," says the first, "for a beer."

"Wade takes a week just licking the pen," says Eben.

"Scuse me, sir," says I. "I can write your letter."

"You, boy?" says Eben. I did not like being called "boy," being a free man now, but as I'm small for my size I let it go.

"I have a fine clear hand," I said.

"Why, there's your man, Eben," says the first. "You can't turn down a fine clear hand."

"And what would be your fee for this?" says Eben.

That was where I realized I mave been a business-man at heart.

"You pervide the pen and ink and paper and postage," says I, "I'll write it for a nickel."

"Nickel's cheap for a good letter, Eben," says the first man.

"Okay, then," I said, "I'll do it for a dime."

"Snap him up, Eben," says the man, "before his price goes through the roof!"

"I'll try you," says Eben. So he gets the necessaries from the store owner, and right there on that barrelhead I despatched a letter in half a trice to his dictation.

April 13, 1860

Mister Nathan Marsh
Greeny Lane
Chelsea, Vermont
United States of America

Dear Nathan,

All is Well. Good dirt. Good grain. Good wives. Get out here.

Your Brother, Eben Marsh.

"Handsome letter," says Eben when I was done. "See there, Vern. A hand you can actually read the letters on, and all in a row!" And he paid me my first dime.

Right there in that store I envested in a pen of my own, a bottle of ink and paper, and some cardboard for a pair of signs to hang on Gabe. One sign said: "Scribe. I Will Write Your Letters If You Cant." The other sign said: "Manuensis For Hire. Epistles Of Ever Nature For Ever Occasion." Rain melted the "e," turning "Scribe" into "Scrib," and so I got my name.

Course, anybody that could read the signs could write their own letters. But it wasn't just ill-letterates who craved my services. There was people like that farmer whose hand was ill-legilible, and others like Romulus who hired me for my poetry and exalted style.

And so at thirteen years of old I become a happy businessman, wending my way westwards. One long year I wandered, following a haphazzard chain of letters till I come to the Hill City district. The first time Romulus Vollmer fed me his collyflowers and scraped out "Beulah Land" on his fiddle, I knew I had found a fit destination and begun my circuit with the town of Hill at the center. Hill also had a post office where I could drop off correspondences ever few weeks. But even now, two years since coming there, I still got visited by my mother practicly ever night in my sleep. She would fade palely into view and gaze on me with sadness but never say a word. Now, I am not pertickly fond of apparitions, but if they're going to appear, I do perfer them to speak their minds.

Yet it wasn't only in my sleep my mother would visit me. Any smell of lavender could choke me up instintly, and I was always aware of her out eastwards someplace, just like I could be aware of the big Canyon without being anyplace near it. My mother followed me by day and night, but I doubt she had stalked me up onto a ridge and smoked a tar-black cigar and left a sign in ashes that said "Die." That was not her style.

Chapter Four
I VISIT WITH A PAIUTE

A fter fleeing Romulus's conflickration, I decided to slip from sight for a while and visit Pierre Trakki, my Injun customer. Pierre moved around a lot, or should I say got moved around a lot, for white folks kept kicking him off their land. At that time he was living out on Demon Butte, a place so bare it made Romulus's ranch look like the Poorly Gates.

Just like always, Pierre looked unsuprized when I appeared. He was scraping out a clay pot, squatting out front of his wickiup, which is what Paiutes use for teepees. It looks like a nest wove out of willow reeds and branches, turned on its side. This wickiup whistled like a flute in the hot high wind that never seemed to let up on that butte. I bet if you stood long enough in that sandy wind, you'd wear away like a cake in a hurricane, but Pierre never seemed to notice it, not even naked as he was.

Pierre would not shook hands with you or ever offer to. First time I met him, I held out my hand and he regarded it like a turd. I once tried saying "Beautiful day, Pierre," and he looked through my head clear to the other side.

Like usual, Pierre went straight to business.

"Did I get an answer?" he said.

"Nothing, Pierre," I said. "Not as yet."

"We'll write again today," he said, and he crouched into the wickiup. I unhitched my writing bag and followed him in.

Now here I was in tight quarters with this Paiute Injun, footsole to footsole, inside his very own wickiup. I had writ half a dozen letters for this man, but I still knew nothing about him. Plus I wondered if he might have some Injun wisdom about my current perdickamint. So whilst I readied my pen I said, "Pierre, you're a Paiute, right?"

Pierre just shrugged.

"Now, Pierre is a French name," I said. "Do you come from the northern Paiutes, up Idaho? Or maybe do you have a little Nez Purse in you?"

He shrugged again.

"Is 'Trakki' like 'Truckee'?" I said. "There's a Truckee in the Sierras. You come from out that way? California?"

He shrugged again.

"You must've spent a fair time among white people to know English so good," I said.

"So *well*," he corrected me. But he still didn't elabberate on the question any.

I said, "Did you fight in the Pyramid Lake War?"

He said, "I don't remember."

"What I don't get is," I said, "that clay pot there is Hopi. And the beadwork on your leather is Navajo. And the fletch on your arrows, that's not Paiute. So what are you, exactly?"

"Injun," he said. "Dip your pen."

Skipping wisdom for the nonce, I dipped my pen and dated a page and put on the usual address, using my roundest hand.

"'To Mr. President Abraham Lincoln,'" I wrote. "'The White House, Washington.'"

"'Dear Sir,'" Pierre said.

"Hold it, Pierre, hold it," I said. "'Dear Sir.' Now, that's not enough for a President of a whole country. Howbout trying a greeting that's got some yeast in it?"

"'Dear Sir,'" he said again.

"Howbout 'O Great White American Lord,'" I said. "That'll rise nicely. Or, 'Most Highest Prince.' Or maybe just: 'Your Majesty.'"

"'Dear Sir,'" he said again.

"Pierre, you have written how many of these letters," I said, "and have you heard one single word in return? Maybe Mr. Lincoln picks up these letters and reads 'Dear Sir' and he throws them away."

Pierre looked like he was thinking that over.

"'Dear Sir,'" he said, and I wrote it down. Truth to tell, I doubted Mr. Lincoln even saw the 'Dear Sir' parts of these letters.

"'I write to you again,'" Pierre said, "'in anger.'"

I stepped in once more.

"Howbout," I said, "'in anger and deep sorrow.' Sorrow's good. It kinda takes the edge off the anger part."

"'In anger,'" he said.

Well, in my experience you can't talk for people. So I wrote down "anger."

"'In all times,'" he went on, "'there are wars. In all times, tribes battle tribes for land or food. But your tribe has started a new kind of war. For you drive all other tribes off the land like animals for slaughter.'"

"'Slaughter' is a powerful word," I said.

Pierre ignored me.

"'Your goverment has taken our land for what it calls protection. Will you pen us up? Will you shut up the wolf and muzzle the bear so that you can feed in safety? Will the coyote win the land?'"

"Now hold it right there, Pierre," I said. "You can't go comparing the white man to a coyote. That's not a argument, that's name-calling. It's sure not gonna get you any ground with the U.S. President."

Pierre took that in and pondered it, then nodded.

"No coyote," he said.

"No coyote," I said.

I scratched out the coyote, and Pierre took back up.

"'Beware,'" he said, "'that your children do not build on land soaked in blood. Do you not see what is happening? And can you not change it?'"

Pierre stopped as if that was the end.

"Your Humble and Obedient Servant," I supplied, but he said, "'Sincerely, Pierre Trakki.'" I wrote it and he put his mark at the bottom of the page, which was this:

I added in at the bottom: "Care of Scrib, Hill Post Office, Hill City District."

I never liked to charge Pierre because he was dirt poor, or sand poor, but he always dug out the coins to pay me. Then he rattled some pine nuts out of a leather pouch for us to share. He might have thought white people was coyotes, but he still shared food with me. Long as people do that, I guess it don't matter what they think of you.

Pierre was a Digger Injun, so my diet had enlarged considerable since meeting him. I had tasted all manner of berries and prairie rice and even the soft parts of cattails. He could hit just about anything with a bow or a spear-thrower, so I had also tasted of muskrat and gila monster and snake and even mouse, which tastes a lot like chicken, but smaller. Everything cept coyote, whose meat a Paiute will never touch. The fact that he was down to some old pine nuts did not say much for the fertility of the land up Demon Butte.

We chewed in silents a while, then I said, "Pierre, somebody's following me."

He looked as suprized as I had ever seen him, which wasn't too much.

"Why," he said.

I said, "I don't know."

"Why are you telling me?" he said.

"Well," I said, "I thought you might have some wisdom."

"Why?" he said, and I wished he'd stop whying me.

I said, "Injuns are sposed to know things we don't."

"Why," he said, right on skedjle.

"Anyways," I said, "somebody's following me."

Pierre said, "Somebody's following everybody."

"Now you see?" I said. "'Somebody's following everybody.' I told you you had wisdom."

He said, "A man was here looking for you."

My heart paused long enough to jump up my throat.

"A black man."

"Did he wear a black hat with a blue band around her?"

Pierre nodded, and my heart jumped up my throat again.

I said, "Maybe now's the time for me to quit being a letter writer and change perfessions. I sure as h——l ain't spendin' my life spillin' ink for a livin'."

Just like always when I pertested too much, I started ain'ting and swearing and dropping my *g*'s, as if that made my lies any more credibible.

"What will you be," Pierre said, "if you're not a letter writer?"

I said, "I kinda thought I'd be a sailor."

Pierre pondered that for a minute in some real thick Injun silents.

"Not much water out here," he said.

"I don't mean out here. My father was a sailor," I said. "Maybe I'll fish for whales."

"You enjoy danger?" he said.

"You don't have to en*joy* danger to be a whale fisherman," I said. "Or maybe I'll set up someplace exotic. Brazil, maybe."

Pierre said, "Where is Brazil?"

I said, "South America."

"Where?" he said.

"Well I don't know where Brazil *is*, Pierre. I seen it on a map." I tried drawing him a map in the air. "We're here, and South America's down here. This is Australia someplace way over here. North Pole's way up at the top. Brazil's kinda . . . in here, somewheres." I stuck my finger at a spot in the oxygin.

"Long way," he said.

"Well, Pierre," I said, getting kinda worked up, "that's the whole *point*, ain't it? I'll tell you what I *don't* want to be. I don't want to be like a century plant, blooming once in seventy-five years and then kicking off. That is not a life."

41

"It is if you're a century plant," he said, and there was no arguing with that. It was pure Injun wisdom.

I never left Pierre without a cartload of things to ponder on, and that visit was no exception. "Somebody's following everybody," for a sample. That was the kind of matter you could philosophate upon for years and never truly figger out. I hardly knew where to begin as I picked my way down the scrabbly side of that butte, but I fergot philosophy entirely as I reached the bottom and looked out over the flat and made out a little twitching burr on the herizon.

Whoever was following me still was. I decided to take jurasstic action to try to lose him.

"Gabe," I said, "I'm sorry to tell you this. We're gonna have to go through the Talking Rocks."

Chapter Five

IN WHICH I VENTURE AMONG THE TALKING ROCKS AND MEET CRAZY JAMES KINCAID

There was a shortcut to the Smeed place that led through the Talking Rocks, but I had always hesititated to go that route. Gabe hesititated too now when I headed him in that direction, but the Talking Rocks was my only path if I was to lose my pursuer. Better people than I have been shaken by that passage. Even Injuns perfer to go round it.

I could discern the Talking Rocks long before I got to them, for they stand in the middle of the scree like a twisted cathedral. Soon the scattered cactus and cacia and mesquite thinned out, and crooked rocks begun to shoot up in my way as if they was plants, first gravestone high, then child high, then man high and tree high. I found myself threading through a blind maze of twisting pillars curled like tongues and fluted with pits like wormholes, as if some stone-eating bug had bored into the rock. Penned on all sides by stone without landmarks, all I could do was ride by the sun. If you couldn't read the sun, you would circle in that labrinth till you thirsted and died. A skeleton still in his snake-skin boots lay grinning at me just past the entrance like a Do Not Enter sign. Gabe stepped back and bawked, but I pressed him on.

It's not the twisty shape of the rocks that makes the place so terrible. It's that they talk to you as you go. Folks say it's wind whistling through those millions of wormholes—cept there's no wind in that maze. The air is so still it's almost stale. The stones must be blown like oboes by some wind or breath from deep inside the earth. Each pillar is like a throat, only it's a throat attached to no person, no body, no head, no soul. It's just throat.

No sooner was I in than—"Hello," somebody breathed right behind me. I whirled around and said, "Who's there?"

Nobody was there, a course. The voice was small and high and child-like, more like a breath than a voice.

"Scrib," a voice said ahead of me, and I whipped back

around, when a voice to my left said, "No, Scrib."

Then something chuckled a deep mean chuckle in my right ear, so close I swatted at it like a horsefly.

I had never seen Gabe so frazzled. He was chomping the bit and snuffling and lifting his lips and showing his teeth and rolling his eyes. He kept trying to back up, too, and I had to force him forwards.

"Tickets, tickets," a voice cried somewheres like a train conductor—or was it saying "pickets, pickets"?

"Swoon," sighed another voice.

"Think!" a voice commanded me. "Think! Think!" But I couldn't think, for the voices was coming faster and faster now, like a crowd of sleepers waking up and realizing I was there. Each voice had only one message to deliver, and cried its message over and over and over.

"Why?" one voice repeated. "Why? Why? Why . . . ?"

"Barber! Barber!"

"My heart," a woman's voice cried. "O my heart."

"Money . . ."

"The moondog. The moondog . . ."

"Where?" one lost voice breathed out again and again. "Where? Where?"

Those circumstances, you got to hang onto your self however you can, and I did so by using the calmingest words I know. Riding on through that invisible choir, I added my own voice over all of theirs.

"'The Lord is my Shepherd,'" I said a-loud. "'I shall not want.'" When he heard those words, Gabe must have realized the point of despairation I had reached. "'He maketh me to lie down in green pastures,'" I cried, but "Where? Where? Where . . . ?" countered that same lost voice over and over.

Once I had recited all the way through the psalm, I started it over again. But the voices multiplied and the racket ratcheted up and the din drowned me out till I had to shout the top of my lungs like a person possessed.

"'THE LORD IS MY SHEPHERD!'"

"Hello, handsome."

"Two-eleven p.m. Two-eleven p.m. . . ."

"Shut the door!"

"'I SHALL NOT WANT!'"

"Cigar?"

"Run, boy, run!"

"Nothing . . ."

"'HE MAKETH ME TO LIE DOWN IN GREEN PAS-TURES!'"

"Bob wire. Bob wire . . ."

"Nothing . . ."

"'HE RESTORETH MY SOUL!'"

"Fix me! Fix me! Fix me!"

"Nothing . . ."

"String him up! String him up!"

"Nothing . . . Nothing . . . Nothing . . ."

One deafening single voice seemed to cry out, "No, no, no!" over and over, and soon I become frantic. I forgot that I knew who I was or why I was riding through there, I forgot I had a mission and a purpose and a letter to deliver, and I cursed myself for venturing into that place. I was hot and hoarse and weary and I begun to tremble, and the psalm of David turned into just another noise amidst the noises, shot ragged of all meaning. I had reached the uttermost dead end of distress.

Then I bruptly realized that I had begun to hear my self again, sounding out solo midst the other voices. The Talking Rocks quieted down gradjle-ly, as if they was dreamers dropping back to sleep, then hummed for a while like a thousand pitchpipes all out of tune, though from time to time I'd still make out a muttered word or two. Soon the stones started to shorten down towards man height again. I tell you, Gabe sure picked up his step as the way begun to clear before us.

"'He restoreth my soul,' all right!" I cried aloud.

"Thank you, King David! Whoo-eee!"

Now, none of this was charicteristic. I am not usually the "Whoo-eee!" type one day out of 365, but I "whoo-eee'd" a few more times just because it felt so good. I even slapped my dusty hat about my knees for joy, some-thing I had never done before in my whole live-long life. I guess danger will make you various, whether you are various by nature or not.

"Say there," said a voice above me, and I stopped slapping my hat.

Crazy James Kincaid was sitting on a rock just over my head. I knew him from all the Wanted posters by his standup hair and his wall eye. The only thing missing was his famed arsinal of 12-shooter pistols. He puffed on a crooked black stogie and studied me serious a minute, wreathed in smoke. I mediately wondered if it was the ashes of one of his stogies that had spellt out "Die" on a certain boulder.

"That's a lotta whoo-ee you're makin' there," said Crazy James Kincaid.

"I'm sorry, sir," I said with a audible gulp. "It ain't typical." I don't know why I felt forced to apologize or explain my character. Maybe it's cause I was petrified.

"Are you the traveling emanuelensis?" he said. His notorious hair stood greased up on end about three or four inches and give him a look of constant mazement.

"Yes, sir," I said.

"Okay," he said. He flicked the butt away and said, "Find your way around. And don't pull any firearms."

I circled round the stone he was on, expecting to find the whole Kincaid Gang, but all I discovered was a wheezy old horse and a yella panting dog sitting in a grotto that looked to be their home. Kincaid dropped down from his rock and stepped up and regarded me close. The smell of old wine clung to him thick as cough syrup. Trouble was, with that wall eye I couldn't tell if he was looking at me or at something else. He seemed to be looking all over the place all at the same time. I was suprized he could fire a gun straight enough to kill as many people as he had. I just hoped he had hit his victims at random, because then I stood a chance of staying alive.

"Welcome," he said. "This here's Esmeralda," and he pointed to that wheezy old horse. He seemed to expect me to say hello to his horse, and I muttered a feeble howdydo. "She's a real steeplechaser."

"Is she, sir," I said, and I noted my voice was none too steady.

"That's Jupiter," he said of the yella panting dog, who looked to be pretty walleyed him self.

"'Lo there, Jupiter," says I, rather faintily.

"I guess you know who I am," he said.

I said, "Yes, sir, I do. You're Crazy James Kincaid."

He said, "What's your name?"

"Scrib, sir," I said.

"Well that's a crazy name," said Crazy James.

"It's a misunderstanding for 'scribe,' sir."

"Okay," he said.

He looked a lot younger than I expected for a man who had been depredating the countryside for fifty years. I still couldn't tell which eye was looking at me, or if he was even looking at me a-tall. That porcupiny hair kept distracting me, too.

"Look in *this* eye!" he shouted in my face, pointing to his left eye. "*This* eye!"

"Yes, sir," I said. My own hair mave stood on end a inch or two.

"Folly," somebody said behind me. "Follicle."

I startled a little and said, "What's that?"

"It's just the rocks," he said. "Don't mind them."

"Pain," said one of the rocks.

"Pleasure," said another.

"Quiet down, rocks!" Crazy James shouted, and I saw why folks called him crazy. Yet those rocks did seem to sulk down to a stony silence after he scolded them.

"You got any writing insterments with you?" he says.

"Yes, sir," I said.

"Okay," he says. "Get 'em and pull up a stone. I want to send a letter."

Chapter Six

I WRITE A LETTER AND AM MURDERED

I unhitched the writing bag and seated my self in the grotto. That yella panting dog was walleyed all right. I bet his left paw never knew what his right one was doing.

"What do you charge for a letter?" said Crazy James.

"For you, sir," I said, "I'll do a letter at no charge whatsomever. A free sample."

"Well, what the h——l kind of businessperson *are* you?" he bust out. His eyes alternicated looking at me, and I tried to favor the left one as commanded. "*Free?*" he said. "Why? Because I'm *crazy?*"

"Oh, no," I baldly lied. "Just genral principles. Human charity."

"Genral principles," he scoffed. "Human charity. I am a citizen of America, where nothing comes free except the people. And I pay good wages for good labor, so you go ahead and charge me like you charge anybody else. Now what's your price?"

I told him a menu of prices and showed him his choice of papers. He picked the 2-cent sunflower-yella paper, maybe in honor of his dog, and a envelope in April Cloud White.

"You charge extra for big words?" he said. "I might use a couple."

"No, sir," I said. "Pit, pinecone, paradise, pollycromatic, you pay the same."

"Okay," he said. I had noticed he said "okay" a lot. "You want some stomach settler?" he said. He held out a mostly empty wine bottle.

I said, "I never touch it, sir."

"It's stomach settler," he said, and I didn't know if it was really stomach settler that just smellt like old wine or if it was old wine that he called stomach settler.

"My stomach's pretty settled already," I lied.

"Okay," he said, and he helped himself to a swig.

"You mind if I ask you a question, sir?" I said.

"Okay," he said.

"Have you been following me since up in the pines?"

"No, I have not."

"Okay," I said.

"Not to my knolledge, anyhow."

"Okay," I said. Now I had also started saying "okay." It's funny how fast you can pick up another people's styles.

"Okay," says Crazy James Kincaid, and puts his boots up to think. "Take a letter."

I readied my pen.

"'Dear Ma and Pa,'" he said, "'and Sister Bea and dear Uncle Tim and Aunt Maggie and Cousin Sedge.' You got that?"

"How do you spell 'Sedge'?" I said.

"I don't know how you spell Sedge!" he said. "Why do you think *you're* writing the God d——n letter?"

"I'll do my best, sir," I said.

"It's short for Sedgwick."

"Yes, sir," I said, and he went on.

"'All is well out here except now I'm wanted for killing a rancher I did not kill. There's 5,000 dollars on my hide now,'" he said. "'What a joke.' You know how to spell joke, don't you?" he said.

"Yes, sir," I said.

"'I sure do miss the farm, but there's no going back. The air out here is so good for my signuses. What with the low humility, I'm hardly sniffling or sneezing a-tall, thank the Lord. However, I lost a tooth last week. The tooth fairy brung me squat for it.'" He chuckled and said to me, "My Pa will laugh at that one. He was always the tooth fairy."

"Yes, sir," I said.

"Were you visited by the tooth fairy as a youngster?"

"No, sir," I said, "my mother didn't go in for it. She called it pagan superstition."

"What about your pa?" he said.

"He was a sailor," I said. "He sank off Brazil."

"Tragic," said Kincaid. "For you were deprived of a real joy."

I couldn't tell which was tragic—my father's death or that I never got to experience the tooth fairy. Now his eyes alternicated staring at the top of my head.

"You ever thought of brushing your hair upwards?" he asked outa nowhere.

I said, "No, sir, I hadn't thought of it too much."

"You want to feel good, you try brushing your head *upwards* sometime," said Crazy James Kincaid. "Put some open spaces betwixt your hairs. That'll blow more fresh air into your skull."

"I'll try it, sir."

"Aerate your brain," he said. "That's what she's there for."

"I will, sir," I promised.

"'Anyway,'" he went on with his letter, "'I'm alive until the buzzards nab me and hang me as they're determined to do. I hope the soy beans is prospring. I love you all. Your fond son, Duane. P.S. Here's something for the jam jar.' Now stick that in with it."

He handed me a wad of maybe twelve or fifteen dollars and signed the letter with a Q, which I guess is the only letter he personally knew. I addressed the envelope, "To the Kincaids. Ephraim Farm. Fayette, Tennessee."

"How do you know I won't steal this money?" I said to him.

"Do you think you'd ask me that if you were going to steal it?" he said.

"No, sir."

"Besides which," he said, "you look like a honest fella. Besides which, I'd find you and kill you."

"Yes, sir."

"I do wish," he said, "you'd stop calling me 'sir.' For Jesus' sake, you're a man, not a God d——n butler."

"What should I call you?" I said.

"Call me Crazy," he said. "But you can call me Duane."

"What's Duane?" I said.

"I am," he said. "James is my criminal incogneedle."

"Okay," I said.

He give me 4 cents for the paper and envelope plus the postage and 50 cents for the letter writing, then tossed in a nickel for the tooth fairy. But after I packed the letter in my saddlebag, I didn't know the ettikit of how to leave. Crazy James sat ruminating on a strip of beef jerky.

"So you didn't kill that rancher up towards Sullivan?" I finally asked by way of conversational gambit.

"No, I did not," he said.

"Was it one of your gang?" I said.

"Do you see a gang here someplace?" he said. He gestured round the empty cave. "There is no gang. There never was a gang. It's all a . . . it's all a . . ."

"Misunderstanding?" I said.

"It's a lie," he said. "It's a slander, it's a label." He bit off some jerky and topped it with a slug of stomach settler. "I come out here for my health and what happens? Suddenly I'm a desperado."

"But you been depredating this countryside for fifty years," I said.

"What'd I do, start before I was born?" he said. "I'm only thirty-four come December!"

I surpressed a urge to wish him happy birthday.

"They just decided to blame me for everything that's gone *wrong* for the past fifty years is all. If a God d——n calf dies, they say I poisoned it. Somebody's apple pie gets burnt, I'm the one left it in the oven too long. They made me six-foot-two on the posters, I'm five eight-and-three-quarters in my boots. How would *you* feel about such lies?"

"Bad," I said.

"Then they go and make up 12-shooters and a whole Kincaid Gang. There ain't no such thing as a 12-shooter pistol! What next? My own private army?"

"But didn't you once shoot a man over a joke you didn't think was funny?"

"I did, but that was a long time ago. And I didn't shoot him because his joke wasn't funny, I shot him because that joke was o-fensive. It was o-fensive to my religion and my country and to womanhood. Also, to yella dogs. And I didn't *kill* him," he said. "I just shot him."

"Okay," I said.

"You don't kill a man over a joke."

"Not usually," I said.

"I'm not crazy, you know," he said. "I'm walleyed."

"Okay," I said.

"People see somebody looks different, they start

making things up and blaming. You imagine what people would say if I was *cross-eyed*?"

"Grievious things, sir," I said.

"*Grievious*, Scrib!" he said. "Don't ever take against somebody because of the way they look, walleyed or elsewise."

"I won't." I recalled a cross-eyed boy in Saint Louis who I had tormented, and I took a moment to regret it.

"But y'know," he said, "if you tell anybody we met here, I might have to shoot *you*."

"I know that," I said. "I won't tell a soul."

"Not even for 5,000 dollars' reward?"

"Privacy's privacy, in my perfession," I said. "I figger a letter writer's like a priest under the trained seals of confession."

"You look like you want to leave."

"I do, Duane," I said.

"Well, nobody's keeping you." He stood up and offered a hand. "Scrib," he said, "I'm glad you passed my way and it was a real treat getting to know you."

"Likewise," I said, and we shook. "Good luck."

As I rode back out the grotto and among the Talking Rocks, Crazy James Kincaid called out to me, *"Aerate your brain!"*

I thought to myself two things. First: *I have met*

Crazy James Kincaid. Second: *I am still alive.* I celebrated them both, but pertickly the latter. Very soon the twisty pillars shrunk back down to child height, then to gravestone height, and the land broke up into gulches and royos and fossies. I descended into the gully of a dried-up river and mazed my way down its twists and turns, breathing easier now than before, for I was safe from my mysterious black-hatted tracker now.

The gully narrowed down almost to a tunnel, and a echo inside it made Gabe's hoofs sound like two horses. I must have gone another mile or so and was riding along happly, still pondering my meeting with Crazy James Kincaid, when I could have swore I smelled some black-tar tobacco . . .

Whoomp! A brick wall slammed into my head from the left side and knocked me clean out my saddle. I came to a moment later on my knees, cocked up on one elbow and looking at little red drops forming on the sand below me. Then I spit out a tooth, and I dimly realized that those was drops of blood and they was coming from the side of my head. *Now that's curious,* I thought. *I'm bleeding.* My head seemed to be full of some kind of loud mortar and I couldn't move my jaw right and I thought I was gonna throw up. I heard a *tching!* behind me and wondered where I had heard that before.

60

Whoomp!

That brick wall slammed into my temple again and knocked me flat out to the side. I rolled up choking and hacking on the dust cloud I'd stirred up and found myself looking at a man closing in on me with a club in his hands, a six-foot length of dead withered tree. Though my head was still full of that loud mortar, I knew enough to jerk away, and when he swung he only grazed my flank. I scrambled on a few feet, but he bore down and swung again. I turned and raised a arm to ward the blow and heard my hand shatter.

The man was a total stranger. He wasn't a black man in a black hat. He was blond and sleek and had a jiggle-o moustache. He wore a suit of dove gray that looked cut to fit him, just like the matching gray kid gloves on his hands. A gold watch chain flashed on his vest.

"Thought you could trick me," he said. His voice was flat and eastern, and in his grisly smile I saw that, like a lot of people from out east, his teeth was rotted from sweets. They was also tarred from tobacco, and I guessed that it was one of this man's smokes that had spellt out the word "Die."

I tried backing off and scrambling straight up the side of the gulch, but he smashed me back down with his club.

"Thought you could slip off through the Talking Rocks," he said. He tossed the club aside and took a barbed whip off his belt that he applied left and right on me, snapping it loud.

"Stop, sir," I said, "stop," but *snap* I felt my left cheek open up, then *snap* the whip lashed my neck on the other side, and *snap* it sliced a chunk out of my head, and *snap* it just missed taking out my left eye. I whirled around to get away from it and *snap snap snap* it opened up the skin down my back, and all this while his spurs rung out *tching tching tching* on the stones. I tried diving out of reach, but *snap* those thongs wrapped my ankle, and he tripped me up onto my face and broke my nose. The barbs lashed across my back a few more times, then the whole confusion stopped and I could hear the man panting hard.

"Look at me," he said.

I rolled around and figgered he was gonna finish his job.

"Do you know me?" he said.

"No, sir," I said.

"Well, you do now. Do you want some advice?"

Those circumstances, there's always only one answer.

"Yes, sir," I said.

"Take another line of work. The one you're in is bad for your health. Pick another territory. Do you hear me?"

"Yes, sir," I said.

"Good," he said, and he stepped up and kicked me hard in the ribs, then he kicked me in the kidneys, then he kicked me right in the heart, and when I crumpled over, he must have kicked me in the head because the sun went out like a blown candle.

Chapter Seven

I FIND I HAVE BEEN CURIOUSLY ROBBED

I come to in the deep of night in some dark cave, naked and shivering, wrapped tight as a Gyptian mummy in a blanket. Somebody groaned misrably nearby and I realized it was me, for every groan I heard made my ribs ache. Some invisible fat boy seemed to be seated on my chest and crushing me.

"Scrib," somebody said. "Hey, Scrib."

Two faces leaned right over me and looked close in my eyes. From a long way off, I reckonized them as the faces of Crazy James Kincaid. I did not know if I had doubled-vision or if I was dead and he *was* a vision. I vaguely realized then that I was in his grotto, for I heard Jupiter panting somewheres by my ear.

I tried saying "water." My lips was dry wool, and nothing come out. He guessed what I wanted and dribbled water out of a canteen onto my lips till some of it found its way down my throat.

Now, getting the hay truly beat out of you is not like it happens in the melodraymas. In "The Hero of the High Country," Jake Masterford gets blindsided by a man with a paper-mashy club, but Jake's no sooner knocked out than he's up on his feet again, pulling a 6-gun and blasting away like the Fourth of July. After I drunk the water Duane give me, I flickered back out and stayed out for a whole nother day. Duane told me afterwards that I hovered during that time betwixt this world and the next. Once, I stopped breathing for a full minute, and Duane thought that I had gone over. Then I sat up and started talking very wild, saying I had to go somewhere, I had a pointment to keep, important letters to write. I kept asking President Lincoln to help me.

When I finally come out of that long sleep, a couple more days passed before I was able to sit up and eat anything. Ever tiny mouthful cut and bumped down through my insides like grit under a eyelid. My head and hair and face was caked with wounds, and one side of my face was purple from forehead to chin. My left eye was shut and the other swoll to Cyclop size. My nose was a whole new shape entirely. That stranger had beat me straight into a diffrent personality. Five of my ribs was broke, the barbed whip had flayed my shirt and skin to a bloody mess, and my writing hand was the size of a oven mitt. My head was still full of that noisy mortar, and I was still seeing two of everthing, like I was in some kinda para-bull about the doubleness of the world. Frankly I was just concussed.

Whilst we ate supper one night, Duane told me how, after the man in the dove-gray suit had killt me, Gabe trotted back to Crazy James's hideout and led him to me down that maze of gullies. I had crawled about a hunderd yards from where that stranger beat me, leaving a trail of blood and chucking up a few times, but I don't remember any of that. Crazy James found me dying amidst blood and vomit and made a pallet and drug me back to his hideaway. Gabe was right there in the grotto listning modestly whilst Duane told how Gabe led him down the royo to find me.

"Gabe," I said. "Old Gabe," and put out my arms. Gabe shied his nose down to nuzzle me, and I embraced my friend's neck, though his hide nearly rubbed what was left of my face off.

"So you never saw this man in gray before?" Duane said.

"Never," I said. "But he sure seemed to know about me. Did he steal my earnings?"

"Nope," he said. "There was 13 dollars and 13 cents in your pocket. All still there."

I said, "So what could he've been after? It's not like I had anything he'd want."

By the light of the fire I saw Duane get a funny look on his face. He lifted his bottle and took a swig of stomach settler.

"You did have something," Duane said. "And he took it."

"What," I said. "What did he take?"

"Well," he said after a minute. "He took your bag."

I just looked at him.

"You mean my writing bag?"

Duane nodded.

"All the letters?" I said. "The inks and stationeries?"

He nodded again.

I said, "Why would anybody want that?"

We had no answers, so we pondered a while in silents together.

"Well," I finally said, "it don't matter since I won't be writing any more letters anyhow."

"There's plenty more ink in the world," Duane said. "There's a whole black ocean of it out there."

"I mean I won't be writing any more letters. I'm getting out of this business," I said. "I'm done. I'm through."

"Why?" he said.

"Why?" I said. "Just look at me! Pursued. Tracked down. Clubbed and whipped. My face is revised. My hand is smashed. My heart hurts. That assassin told me to take another perfession and so I will. I'll go into something safe—like milking rattlers for venom, or hunting grizzly bears."

I was suprizing myself with the force of my own explosion.

"I'm sorry he got your family's jam-jar money," I added in.

"I can't blame you for losing a letter you got beat up in the losing of," Duane said. "But what about all those other people's letters?"

"I don't care," I said.

"But you're a damn fine emanuelensis," he said. "You was born and breaded for words."

"Where did words ever get me?" I said. "Fifty cents a page and beat up worst than the Good Samaritan."

"Scrib," he said, "there's occupational hazards to everthing. Even letter writing. So I wouldn't take this beating too personal. But the day you admit the truth about your self to your self, that's a great day for any person. The day you admit what you really are deep down. And I say you're a scribe. I say words is your calling and ink is your elemint like peppermint to a candy-maker. A course, I'm sayin' all this for selfish reasons. For how'm I gonna talk to my kin in Tennessee without somebody like you? How's a person's father or mother gonna tell the rest of the world they been born? Seems to me there's some secret force, some great invisible War that keeps people divided and separate and scattered over the face of this earth. But you, Scrib, you connect people up like dots on a puzzle. And what are you gonna do with your life or your self that's more nobler than that?"

"I said I don't care," I said, "and what I mean is, *I don't care!*"

I was so het up that right then and there I got up and tore my Scribe signs off Gabe and tossed them into the fire at the mouth of the cave. They was flames in a instant. Duane stared at them burning up as if he had been slapped, and when they floated into the sky as two black wings of weightless ash and disappeared, he shook his head and let out a doleful sigh.

"Okay, Scrib," he said without heart. "I say it's still too bad."

"Too bad is too bad," I said, which is the kinda foolish

empty argument a person can come up with when he's wrong. Yet my voice was shaky, and I felt like I was about to bust into tears. "And now I'm going to sleep."

We didn't talk about it again. Some days after that, we shook hands and parted. I had already decided where I was headed—out of the dangers of the circuit and into the safeties of town. I would live the good life, enjoying all the eumenities.

Course, nothing ever works out like you expect. Nothing that matters, anyhow. By which I mean my troubles was still far from over.

Chapter Eight

EPISTOLARY

Here is some of the letters that got stole from my bag:

To Miss Edwina Maww
PO Box 6
Bellevue, Kansas

Dearest Edwina,

How are you. I'm real fine except for a
pain in my shoulders day and night and
the old ache in my leg where that
spaniel bit my calf off. My elbow is still

swoll. My left ear has begun to itch lately. Did I mention I am losing my hair? Well, I am. My stool is all hard black pellets lately but I don't complain. How are you and your ringworm?

Your sister,
Virginia Slakely

P.S. The green salve didn't work. Please send some more and your recipe for peach crumble.

To Mr. Richard Dix
Excelsior Tool Company
186 State St.
Chicago Illinoise US of A

Dear Sir,

I say you're a liar and your products are HORSE MANURE.

Angrily,
C. T. Gelles,
Blacksmith

Señora Maria Vasquez
Avenida Temblador
Juarez, Mexico

Adorada Madre,

Papa ha muerto.

> *Tu hijo eterno,*
> *Pedro*

Head Philosopher
Oxferd University
Oxferd England

Dear Sir or Ma'am,

I am a wife and mother of 6 but I have lately come to the idea that none of us is really here and this world is just a dream. What do you make of this? You're suppose to be smart.

> Inquiringly,
> (Mrs.) Clarence Witherspoon

Colonel Everett Frame
Army of the Confederate States of America
Near Atlanta Georgia

Dear Colonel,

This is to say your animals are all fine. The sheep
are fine and the goats are fine and Quinsy has
birthed. I hope the war is well and you are having
a fine time. Kill a few Yankees for me.

Signed,
Zeke

Karl and May Ludendorff liked to write letters to their
daughter Katrina out loud together, only they changed
and corrected and rethought each other so much,
pacing around their kitchen table scratching their
heads, after a while I stopped crossing out the changes
and just left the whole stew. Here, for a sample, is the
resulting mess:

Dear Dearest To our dear sweet To our Darling
Dear Katrina,

How are you. We hope, pray, hope and pray you

74

are fine, feeling well, feeling fine, doing all right, good. Everything here is, everything out here is, everything back home is, we're both fine, good, feeling fine, feeling well, doing all right ourself. And how is that no-good so-called husband of, how is your, how is Kurt? I hope he ~~rots~~, we hope he is doing fine, all right, we hope and pray and hope, he's, Kurt is good, well, okay. The cat kicked off, died, is dead, passed away last week, the other week, two weeks, some time ago, I'm we're sorry to inform, tell you, say. Well, Kitty was decripit, old, sick, old and sick, pretty sick, getting on, ready to kick it anyhow. ~~Father put her in a sack,~~ Father was there at the end, finish, last moments, final end. That's about it, all, it, everything we have to say, all the news, everything, it, for now, today, now, honey, sweetie, daughter.

Love and kisses, kisses and hugs, love and hugs and kisses, all our love,

> Your Parents, Momma and Poppa, Karl
> and May Ludendorff, You Know Who

There was another dozen letters in that bag, each as different as these. Like I like to say—people are various.

Chapter Nine

I TRY THE GOOD LIFE
AND FAIL MISRABLY

I don't know who named the town of Hill, but there is no hill for miles around Hill. There is not a knoll nor a knob nor so much as a sizable anthill. Maybe the founder of Hill's name was Hill. Or else he was a real salesman. You got to admit, a city named Hill is more likely to draw than a city named Flat.

In truth, Hill City was going the other way: it was starting to sink. Ever day a couple huge sinkholes would pop open and lower the town a few feet. Main Street was a mess of potholes so big they didn't just slow down traffic, they sometimes swallowed the stagecoach. Some buildings, the second-story windows had descended to eye level. The whole settlement was tilted towards the worst, and even the flattest roofs in Hill was as steep as the prices. The First Church of Hill was sloping so bad, the nave was pitched like a theayter. The congregation sat face-upwards to Heaven in their pews whilst sliding slowly backwards into the Pit. The town was subsiding like sand in a hourglass, but I guess folks can get used to anything, even gradjle disaster.

When I rode into Hill, I wasn't seeing double anymore, but I still couldn't take a full breath without feeling a rib was gonna pop like a busted barrel stave. I didn't mind that, because I was starting a whole new life with 13 dollars and 13 cents in my britches. Frankly there was a couple too many 13's in there for me to feel easy, but I wasn't going to let any pagan superstition bother me. A man could live well on 13 dollars and 13 cents in Hill, and a real man I was going to be, boy no longer.

It's a fine feeling, riding into a metropolis of a morning. The shop windows of Hill was packed with wares, and everplace you looked something was being hawked or sold or bartered. Lavish ladies with money-filled ridicules was out strolling and shopping in bustled droves. A War veteran with no legs went spidering by on two low crutches, fluttring somewhat leafily, for he was peddling lottery tickets pinned all over him like flags. Mr. Dawson stood in the window of his bank, polishing his pince nays, and when he put them on their lenses flashed like coins. A sash flew open in the top story of the Hill Hotel and a maid shook a pee-colored sheet out the window, letting fly all manner of trash and raining down a hailshower of cigar butts on my hat. She had to be the homeliest maid west of China, but she flashed a smile at me and gained in beauty tenfold, despite of her missing teeth, and I waved her my hat, shaking off the cigar butts. Everwhere you looked was Wanted posters with the face of the local arch criminal, Crazy James Kincaid and his gang, which made me laugh inwardly, knowing the atchel truth. There was noise, there was ladies, there was free enterprises and a three-decker hotel with a maid to smile at you, and six whole restaurants, each one with a different menu. I had reached a earthly Heaven.

"Where you headed, Scrib?" a jowly voice called out to me as I rode my way around the potholes on Main. "Dropping off your wares at the Post Office?"

"Morning, Sheriff," I said, and hauled up.

It was Sheriff Ackelberg, picking his teeth out front of the jail with his engraved silver toothpick as if he had just et a coupla fat prisoners for breakfast. The Sheriff always wore that toothpick at a crooked angle as if to rhyme himself with the crookedness of the town as a whole. He pointed to where my signs used to hang on Gabe. "Where's your advertising?"

"I don't need those signs no more," I said.

"Why?" he said. "You rich already?" He laughed at that idea, and his big gut shook like jellied aspic.

"Not rich," I said, "I'm retiring out of that business and setting up here."

"Hill can use a smart boy, Scrib," he said.

"That's good," I said, "cept I ain't 'Scrib' anymore. Cause I ain't writin' no more d——n letters." Here I wasn't two minutes in town and I was ain'ting already and double negativizing and dropping my *g*'s and swearing. "You can call me Billy."

"Okay, Billy," he said. "Say, what happened to your face? You run into some banditos?"

"I fell the wrong way," I said.

"If the boardinghouses are full up, you can always move in here." He winked at me and jerked a thumb back at the jailhouse. "I'll give you a room."

"Thanks, Sheriff," I said, "maybe I'll take you up."

He went off to arrest a blind War veteran tapping by with a tin cup. The streets of Hill was remarkably free of miscreeants because Sheriff Ackelberg kept a clamp on quality-of-life crimes like public charity.

Farther along, another voice stopped me, high and wheezy.

"Scrib! Scrib, wait up!" This was Frank the Postmaster running out the Hill Post Office and chasing me with a mail sack. Usually I would have stopped off at the P.O. first thing, to drop off and collect correspondences. Folks called Frank "Yabbit," cause he was always saying "Yeah, but . . . Yeah, but . . ."

"I got a whole sack of letters for you, Scrib," Frank said.

"Your regular man will have to deliver them," I said. "I'm out of that business, Postmaster."

"Yabbit," Frank said, "I got all this mail here."

"I ain't Scrib no more, I'm Billy now," I said.

"Yabbit," he said, "these letters are all addressed 'Care of Scrib, Hill Post Office.' It ain't legal for nobody to take 'em cept you."

"Then I guess those letters will have to sit," I said.

"Say, what happened to your face?" he said.

"I fell the wrong way."

"Yabbit, Scrib," he said, "there's one *pertickler* letter here I think you better see. . . ."

"I'm Billy now," I said. "And I'll be at the saloon."

Before Frank could yabbit me again, I rode on and stabled Gabe at Grady's, then walked back to the

Golden Eagle. I was about to push through the swinging doors of that illoostrious tavern when a hand grasped my arm.

"Scrib!" a voice said. "Well met, young man!"

"Morning, Your Honor," I said.

It was Oliver McGuinness, the Mayor of Hill, in his pink face and patent-leather shoes and velveety suit and rose bootaneer.

"I bid you welcome," he said, grabbing my hand like a lost ballot. "Our Sheriff tells me you're immigrating." His white moustache was waxed up into two curling question markers, which he liked to twiddle quizzickly. "A wise choice for a smart young consumer. What are your plans?"

"I don't rightly know yet," I said.

"I am a man of the world," he said, "and I say unto you: *Take*, young Scribbler. Take!"

"Atchley, I'm Billy now, sir."

"Take, Billy!" he said, and leaned in close. "You have money?" he said.

"Oh yes, sir."

"Then Hill City can offer you . . . *everything*! You do know the purpose of life," he said as if I did.

"No, sir," I said.

"The Pursuit of Worldly Pleasure. Excess of Senshal

Intoxication. Say, what happened to your face?" he said.

"I fell the wrong way."

"Behold, boy," he proclaimed.

With one hand holding my shoulder he waved his other at the vista before us, which was a fertilizer enterprise across the way. Just at that moment a pothole popped open right in front of us with a suctional sound, about a yard wide and deep enough for a man to stand in. The Mayor was un-phazed.

"People talk of sinkholes," he said. "I prefer to think of those openings as Mines. Diamond Mines, proffering their treasure!" He pressed my hand fervently again. "Young William, I say unto you: *Enjoy!*"

With that, he pushed me through the swinging doors of the Golden Eagle.

The Eagle was full up as always, for Hill stands at a crossroads, and you had men thirsting towards that saloon from all four points of the compass. Any hour of night or day, the legion of brass spittoons around the place rung out like chimes on Easter. I took a stool at the bar.

"Say there, Scrib," says Fly the barkeep. "What are you doing in here?"

"I'll have a whiskey," I said, "and call me Billy."

"Who's Billy?" says Fly.

"I am," I said. "I'll have a whiskey."

"We don't serve boys, Billy," Fly says. "Them's the rules, so go on off."

"I ain't a boy," I said. "I'm a man."

"Boy says he's a man, he's a man," pertests a customer leaning like Pisa down the bar. "Pour for the man, Fly."

I clinked a silver dollar on the bar. "Take it out of that. And there's more where it come from."

Fly regarded the coin. It was so shiny, George Washington was reflected inside-out on Fly's face.

"Rules was made to be broke," Fly says. "What kind of whiskey do you want? We got a selection of single malts, we got a fine peaty Irish label, we got a husky aromatic sour mash with a wheaty afterbite and a trace of raspberry. . . ."

"Sounds fine," I said. "And give me a ceegar."

"Penny or two penny?"

"Whole hog," I said.

"Say, what happened to your face?" says Fly.

"I fell wrong," I said, getting real tired of being asked.

A woman appeared at my side through the tobacco

fog. I reckonized her as Suzi Generous, the town's short answer to the long question of love.

"Morning, cowboy," Suzi said. Her teeth was scarlet. "You're out drinking early."

"When a man needs a drink," I pernounced rather feebly, "he needs a drink."

"It's truth," she said. "And a woman could drink a drink herself right now."

"One for the lady, Fly," I said.

"I hear you're carrying a lode of loose silver," Suzi said.

"Word filters fast," I said.

"Say, what happened to your face?" she said.

I settled for: "Fell."

Suzi laughed. "Who'd you fall into?"

I looked around and saw that everbody around was eavesdropping on our teat-a-teat. Fly made like he was wiping the bar.

"Give him another, Fly," Suzi said. "The man's thirsty."

I said to her, "You know you got lipstick on your teeth?"

She said, "I'll let you lick it off, for a price."

I didn't know what to say, as I couldn't tell if that was

a hard offer. Given my experience was limited to kissing two girls, only one successfully, I wasn't sure if women like Suzi Generous really did let you lick the lipstick off their teeth for money and if that's what men regularly did. The annatomical details was dim. I just knew she was in the Senshal Intoxication business. The wheaty whiskey with a trace of raspberry wasn't helping me line up my thoughts in single file, neither.

"Say, are you Scrib?" Suzi says. "The letter writer?"

"Nope," I said. "I'm Billy."

"Will you write a letter for me?" Suzi says.

I said, "Will you take me up to the Hill Hotel and pervide some Senshal Intoxication?"

I could have swore there was a explosion of laughter around me, but when I looked around everbody was staring into their drinks. That saloon looked so contemplative you woulda thought the men was monks.

"About this letter," she says.

I said, "Forget letters. You are a Lady Of The Night, aren't you?"

"There's no need to get like that," she said.

I said, "A minute ago you was offering to let me lick your teeth."

"I resent this Lady Of The Night stuff," she said.

85

"Does it look like night time to you? This here is broad daylight we're in."

Now a man steps between us and spits out a long brown eel of tobacco spit.

"This boy bothering you, Suki?" he says.

"Her name is Suzi," I said.

The man took that personal somehow and swung at me, smashing me right in the ceegar. I fell back against my rear neighbor, who dominoed into the next man, who took this pretty personal too. The two men swung at each other like wind-up toys, then everbody in the whole place started swinging as if somebody had blowed a whistle to start a beat-up-your-neighbor competition.

In barroom brawls in the melodraymas, people brain each other with chairs that break over their heads and they go flying into mirrors and they shatter bottles in each other's faces and everbody keeps on getting back up and heading back into the fray. Well, outside the melodraymas, it's not quite so pretty. Plus, a couple dozen upturned spittoons had bucketed over the floor, so the poojilists was all swinging and sloshing in a sea of spit and sawdust that they churned into a frothy brown oatmeal.

A coupla gunshots stopped the whole thing cold. It was Sheriff Ackelberg standing in the doorway, firing into the ceiling. Splinters rained down and a shot cat died with a awful screech on the second floor.

"What the h——l is going on here!" the Sheriff boomed. Midst the smashed-up furniture, men was groaning and swearing and wishing they had never come into the world.

"It was Billy," said Fly.

"Billy who?" the Sheriff said. "Who's Billy?"

Fly pointed at me. I was betrayed.

"You did all this, Scrib?" the Sheriff said to me.

"No, sir," I said. "Not exactly."

"You just *got* here," the Sheriff said. "Didn't I just see you ride in?"

"Get that boy out of here," Fly says. And to me he says, "You ever come back in here, I'll break the other side of your face."

"Come on, Billy," Suzi said. She was pretty mussed up, and her dress was soaked in beer and broken glass and hemmed with spit. She grabbed my hand and led me out past the Sheriff, who chewed his silver toothpick fiercely at me as I went by. I could tell he had stopped liking me.

"Watch yourself, boy," he growled.

Suzi steered me through the crowd that had gathered outside and marched me across the street to the Hill Hotel. In the lobby she didn't even stop at the front desk.

"Anybody wants to know," she says, heading me up stairs, "I'm in Number 33."

A clerk in a black eyeshade was sorting mail into pigeonholes. "Okee dokey, Sue," he said without turning round.

The Hill Hotel smelled like rodents. Fact, while we was going up, a greasy-looking rat scuttled right ahead of us along the baseboard like a porter showing us to our room, then ducked through a door-crack into a room. It was Number 33.

The chamber had just space enough for a narrow bed and a deal bureau and a chair and a couple hooks on the wall. It didn't smell like rodents. It smellt like nausea. The rat slipped under the bed.

"So where you from originally?" I said. "Is Suzi Generous your real name?" This was partly to stall, and partly to give that rat a chance to leave graciously.

"My name," Suzi said, "is fifty cents. In advance."

I dug out four dimes and two nickels. She waved

them with her chin onto the bureau. I set them in a quiet stack.

"You sure you don't want to write me that letter?" she said. "You can take it in trade."

"I ain't writing any letters," I said. "I'm pursuing Worldly Pleasures and Senshal Intoxication."

"Okay," she said. "It's your choice." Then the door opened behind me and somebody cracked me on the head with a blackjack, and I fell right on my face into the floor.

Chapter Ten

HAVING BEEN ROBBED AGAIN, I PERPARE TO LIVE A MORAL CIVILIZED LIFE

My eye was swoll back up to Cyclop size and I was seeing double again by the time I came to. Suzi was gone, the rat was gone, my money was gone, 13 cents and everthing. My boots and my belt was gone, too. I was flabbergasted I still had my shirt and my hair.

A cockroach led me back down to the lobby. Seeing doubled like I was, fumbling down two stair-cases at once and gripping the banisters, I must have looked like a blind man with a seeing-eye insect out front of me.

"Hold it there," somebody snapped as I started out the lobby door. It was the clerk in the black eyeshade, split into two. Him and his twin brother was still sorting letters into pigeonholes. "That'll be 40 cents," they said.

I stupidly said, "What?"

"40 cents," the clerks said, "for the use of the room."

I tried focusing on one of the clerks.

"Are you drunk?" they said.

"No," I said, "I'm concussed." I didn't want to tell those clerks about being robbed. It was too shameful.

"You're what?" they said.

I said, "What time is it?"

"What does it matter what time it is," they said, and threw down two stacks of letters. "It's You-Owe-40-Cents Time."

I searched for a lie, but it eluded me.

"I don't have 40 cents," I said finally. "I got robbed."

"When?"

"Just now."

"Where?"

"Upstairs in this hotel," I said.

"You can't tell me you got robbed in this hotel." The two clerks doubled out to four now, and the four doubled to eight, till I had a whole church choir of clerks staring at me insulted. "Nobody gets robbed in the Hill Hotel."

"Well," I said, "then I have started a new tradition."

"40 cents," they said. "Or elsewards."

"I don't have it. I got nothing, and what are you gonna do about it?" I said. "It's your hotel. I'm the one who should be complaining. Do you see me complaining?"

"*Sheriff!*" the choir sang out. A whole posse of Ackelbergs swarmed in the front door and filled up the room.

"What's the problem," the Sheriffs said, and then they saw me. All of my hearts sank.

"This boy is drunk," the clerks said. "He took some woman upstairs, now he won't pay his bill."

"How much," the Sheriff said.

"40 cents."

"I don't have it," I said.

"You don't have 40 cents?" the Sheriff said quietly. He slid the silver toothpick out the slot in his teeth, which seemed a bad omin. Not having 40 cents in Hill was a high crime and mistymeaner.

"I was robbed upstairs," I said. "I was hit on the head and robbed of all my money, and my belt and my boots. You see?" I showed him my stocking feet and how I was holding up my britches by hand. "I had 13 dollars and 13 cents this morning, now I've got nothing. Cept I'm looking at about ten of you right now."

"I told you he was drunk," said the clerks.

"Scrib," said the Sheriffs, real quiet. "You never had 13 dollars, did you."

"I did," I said. "Hard-earned."

"You never had 13 cents. Or a belt. Or boots."

"I did," I said. "Ask at the Eagle."

"Probly stolen money and stolen goods, too," says the clerks. "Jail him, Sheriff. I'll sign a complaint."

That was when I noticed those clerks was wearing my stolen belt.

"Well, there's my belt right there!" I said, and that was when I noticed the Sheriffs was all wearing my boots.

"Come along, Scrib," the Sheriffs said, and they took my arm.

"I been robbed," I said as the Sheriffs hauled me out the door. "And you're sposed to lock up the thief," I yelled, "not the victim!"

It had taken me but two hours in Hill to turn from a letter writer into a saloon-going, hoor-buying, ceegar-smoking barroom-brawl-inciter and to get blackjacked, robbed, unbelted, unshod, and publicly humiliated. I obviously had some kinda talent. I just wished I had a different one.

"Now go on," the Sheriff says, and pushes me off

down the street, "and don't cross me again."

Holding up my britches by hand, I stood in the sun pondering my fate and my choices anew. I knew one thing sure: Dissipation and Worldly Pleasures had got me noplace.

I did on the spot what all cowards historicly do in such situations: I decided to reform. I would lead a peaceful uneventful life as a civilized moral townsperson. And so I started renewedly upon my way, heading up the street in my socks.

Needle-less to say, I was headed further hellwards.

The general store in Hill was a four-story bee-heemoth called The Spicer Emporium, with a vast sign that said "We Vend Everything." The Emporium did vend everthing right up to your fanciest dreams, and at fancy prices to match. At fancy names, too. At Spicer's "clothes" was "apparel," and you never "bought" anything, you "purchased" it, with "tender" not "money." "Food" was "foodstuffs," "feed" was "provender," "fruit" was "produce," "ketchup" was "condiment," "candy" was "confectionery," and "furniture" was "movables" whether they moved or not.

"Salutations, Scrib," Mr. Spicer said with a little bow when I walked in. "Or is it 'Billy' now, as I apprehend?"

All them foodstuffs he vended kept Mr. Spicer

roundly well-provendered. The skin on him was tight and shiny as a blown-up bladder. He wore a straw hat and a apron with the Spicer loco on it: a eye-filling cornealcopia spilling over with buyables.

"Fresh out of nibs?" he said. "A pint of India ink? I have a new French paper. Sleek as Chinese silk, hardy as vellum."

"No, sir," I said. "I want a job."

"A job?" he said. "You mean a 'situation'?"

He was taken aback, for I wasn't after something he could sell me, I was after something that might cost him. Mr. Spicer's eyes toted me up like a bill.

"A clark, eh." He pronounced clerk "clark" because he had heard that British folks do that.

"You always say," I said, "if I ever want to settle down, you'd have a job for me. Well, I'm ready to settle. And," I added, "it'd be the greatest honor of my life to work for you at the Emporeeum."

"Done!" he said. "I'll give you a position at, shall we say, 3 dollars per week?"

"Thank you, sir," I said.

"Minus," he said, "10 cents a week for the rental of your Spicer Emporium uniform. It seems," he noted, "you also need a trouser strap." He noted where my belt had been till recently. "And some footware."

He handed me a belt and a pair of boots off a shelf. "I'll deduct these from your first year's wages. Where are your quarters?"

"I don't have a quarter, sir," I said. "I got robbed."

"Where are you *quartered*?" he said.

"I haven't found a place yet," I said.

"How fortooitous!" he said. "Eugenia and I have a chamber in our very own domicile which I will sublease to you, with board, no lunch, for a dollar fifty per week, sheets and linens not included."

"I'll take it, sir."

"By George, it's my lucky day," said Mr. Spicer, shaking my hand. Somehow I got the feeling he had made a thousand dollars off me. "Betake yourself to my place of residence and tell Eugenia. You commence your duties at rosy-fingered dawn."

I followed the slopey streets of Hill to the Spicer house, which was real grand but deeply sunk, for the richer section of town was pertickly proned to sinkholes. You had to walk down five steps just to get up to the Spicers' front porch. It shook me a little when I saw that a white picket fence circled the house, but spite of this omin I did not flee. I rung the bell and Mrs. Spicer opened the door. Her moustache had really bushed out since my last visit.

"*Mister* Scrib!" she cried as if she had been waiting ten years for me. She never could bear to call me just "Scrib," she always had to Mister me. "What a serene pleasure! Vespasia!" she called. "Come see who has graced our domeysile with his presence!"

Vespasia Spicer, eighteen years old and 180 pounds, popped round a corner, then floated towards me on her hoopskirts like she was on rollers. The Spicers was a large family, making up in size what they lacked number, with probly 8 hundertweight amongst them. The two ladies fillt their frocks like sponge cakes.

"Oh, Mr. *Scrib*," Vespasia smirked at me evacuously, taking my hand. Vespasia wore a sorta permanent smirk, as if the two of you shared some dirty secret she hadn't let you in on yet.

"On-*tray*, Mr. Scrib!" said Mrs. Spicer. "This is our at-home day."

That mave been their day to receive company, but I was all the guests who'd showed up. They floated me into the parlor, where refreshments for about twenty people was spread out amongst the nicktnackts. What with us being below ground level, the room was fairly dark and tomb-like. The funeereal effect was encouraged by the wormy smell, and the fact that all the windows looked out on roots and dirt. Ever now and again a mole would pass by and look in, then retreat as if he didn't like what he saw. Mrs. Spicer bobbed to a sofa and Vespasia air-ballooned over to a divan, which left me to a needle-pointed throne betwixt them. You never saw so much needlepoint if you lived a hunderd years. On the mantel was even a copy of *The Pilgrim's Progress* in a needle-pointed cover. Spite of all these further omins, I did not flee.

"We call this room," Mrs. Spicer said, "our conversation pit."

Well-thumbed copies of *Entertainment Hourly* was flung about the side-tables. Hill had no newspaper as such, but it did have *Entertainment Hourly*, a hand-me-out that listed local events and reviewed everything from shoot-outs to sermons to the minstrel shows at the Palindrome. The town dentist passed out copies to unaesthete his patients when he drilled their teeth. All the town's political news ended up in *Entertainment Hourly*, so a election didn't so much get reported as get rated. You might see a headline like "Hermione Bletchley Elected Town Secretary (Four Stars!!)," or maybe "City Council Passes Trash Bill (B+)." If a wagon got swallowed in a sinkhole, *Entertainment Hourly* would probly say "New Sinkhole Tragedy! Four People And A Horse Dead! Two Thumbs Up!" The family of the victims would probly frame that page, too. Getting your name in *Entertainment Hourly* was the sinny qua non of sellebrity.

"What kind wind blows you to us?" Mrs. Spicer said, and before I could answer she exclaimed, *"Let's eat!"*

"Anchovy paste?" Vespasia said, and held out a fishy cracker towards me.

"Tea?" said Mrs. Spicer, and handed me the world's smallest cup.

"I just et," I lied. "Thanks anyways."

Having conversed with me sufficient, Vespasia and her mother got down to their real business, which was feeding. The way they tucked into the canapees you woulda thought tomorrow had been cancelled. I didn't even have to make conversation, just spectate while they shoveled. After they'd emptied the plates and daintly licked the crumbs off their fingertips, Mrs. Spicer said, "You haven't told us to what we owe this honor."

I explained the deal I made with Mr. Spicer for a chamber in their domicile.

"Mother," Vespasia said, "we have a boarder! What opportunities for social intercourse!"

Mrs. Spicer didn't look so thrilled. "Hmp!" she said. "And what's my good-for-nothing husband charging you?"

I quoted the price and put her at ease. "A fine deal," she said, and I felt like I had just handed the Spicers another thousand dollars. "Arthur!" she called.

A sulky young man in a suit had moped into the doorway. His eyes was dark-ringed and baggy, and he wore his hands deep in his pockets. He looked like he was scratching his knees from inside his trousers.

"Mmm fmm fmm," he said.

"Mr. Christmas, my son, Arthur Junior," Mrs. Spicer said.

"How do," I said.

"Mmm fmm fmm," he said, and moped back out the doorway.

"If you have eaten an elegant sufficiency, Mr. Christmas," Mrs. Spicer said, "we'll show you your lodgment."

The ladies levitated me up two flights to a attic, where Mrs. Spicer opened a narrow door upon a dark and cluttered compartment.

"Broom closet," I said. "Very handsome."

"That," she said, "is your *room*, sir!" And she laughed as if I had made the finest joke. Looking closer I finally made out a cot amidst all the lumber and leavings and dead brown beetles belly-up inside. "Till our evening prandium, then. Toodle-oo!"

She floated down the stairs, and Vespasia oiled up her earnestest smirk.

"Mr. Christmas," she said, "I do look forward to your . . . company." And with that, she bruptly kissed me on the lips and smilt in a way that chilled all my marrows. *"Welcome,"* she said, and deflated down the stairs.

It sure had been a rich and full day.

Chapter Eleven

IN WHICH THE MORAL LIFE FINDS ME WANTING, AND VICE-A-VERSA

ow I sunk still deeper and became downright shameful, for I turned into a wage slave. Six days a week I rose at dawn and put on a Spicer's straw hat and apron and vended items of apparel and unmovable movables and pre-whited white pickets till nightfall, when I locked myself in my broom closet to scape from Vespasia, who crept up ever night and laid siege to my door like a catapult. Luckly I could hear her corsets creaking all the way up. Twice a day at breakfast and dinner I indured Mrs. Spicer discussing the latest fashions coming out of Oklahoma City while Arthur Junior stared into his plate as if it was his grave. Pretty soon I started dreaming in needlepoint, and the dreams was not pretty. I sunk so low I caught myself reading *Entertainment Hourly* by the hourly.

Monday night was the Canasta Club, Wednesdays was the Cribbage Society, and Friday nights was the Literary League, which I attended with a beevy of Mrs. Spicer's lady friends. There, folks would strike a pose and recite things like, "O Death, Death, Death, thou feathery pillow, when shall I lie dead, dead, dead beneath yon willow," then eat vanilla fudge. Sundays I went to church and sung hymns and heard out the sermon by Reverend Bunce, to whom I delivered a gallon of sour mash whiskey ever Monday morning wrapped in a package marked "Dairy Products." I did all this for 3 dollars a week minus room and board and uniform rental and a few other deductions like soap and towel fees, rug insurance in case I wore down the carpets, and a room tax. My first week I came out 35 cents to the good. My second week I had to pay a nickel. Any time I wanted friendly conversation, I went down to Grady's stable and sat with Gabe. He didn't seem to be making any friends himself. And ever day Frank the Postmaster stopped me in the street with that sack of mail and said, "I've still got this mail for you, Scrib. And

there's one *pertickler* letter here I think you oughta see."
I would tell him once again that I was out of the letter-writing business.

Maybe worst of all, I become a addict. Some people are dope fiends or drunkers. I was a ink fiend. Ever night in my broom closet, I could not keep my self from nibbing up a pen and dipping into the deep dark blue ink bottle. Having no letters to write, I would cover sheets of paper with conversations I overheard at the shop or things I'd noticed about the town. I even started stealing ink and paper from the Emporium to feed my habit. This is all plain pathetic, but like I say, we are in the shameful part of my tale.

Trade was brisk at the shop, and you never would have known there was a War on someplace. It was all buy buy buy. But then, in a town tipped as percariously as Hill, folks will naturally seek purchase. It took me but a day to find out the Spicer income mostly come from dirty French postcards kept in a locked drawer behind the counter, depicting what I guess was French people in all sorts of contortions and states of nudidity, looking pretty joyless about it. It was practicly enough to put you off the subject altogether.

Then one afternoon I was in the storeroom looking

for our new preemium beer-keg spigot when I heard a sound that stopped my heart.

Tching.

I prayed that I had heard wrong.

Tching. Tching. Tching.

The rattle of spurs. Whoever was wearing those spurs had come into the shop and was crossing the floor. I climbed a ladder to where I could look down into the shop over the back wall of shelves, and peered betwixt a coupla demijohns.

"A box of my usual panatellas, if you please."

The man in the dove-gray suit was standing at the counter tugging off his handmade kid gloves finger by finger. He looked as he had when he'd been murdering me in that gully, but without the murdrous look on his face. Fact, he looked like a born gentleman, and if you'd seen him in the street you would have tipped your hat and given him the walk.

"Any other items, Mr. Dexter?" says Mr. Spicer, putting down a box of tar-black cigars. "Some fresh habiliments?"

"Perfume," says the man in gray, who I now knew was named Dexter. "Something for a fair lady."

Having degloved him self, Dexter took out a solid-green roll of money that made Mr. Spicer bust out in a pomade-like sweat.

"Certainly, Mr. Dexter. We have a wide selection of à la mode aromas," says Mr. Spicer, and leads this Mr. Dexter into the farther room.

My legs was trembling on the ladder step. It seemed there was no getting away from this assassin, shrink myself small and hide as I might. My first instink was to flee without even collecting my belongings, just leave town and take off. Then I thought, *Scrib*—and I did not call my self Billy now, I called my self Scrib again—*you can live out the rest of your life hiding in some hole or you can look into this*. And then my self went on, *Your father faced the heartless sea day upon day. Mazewell face up here and do what he mighta done, come sink or swim.* Truth to tell, I had found life as a upstanding citizen pretty excretiating anyhow. If I stayed on my present course, I would turn into Arthur Spicer Junior The Second, with my hands permanently poked in my pockets and staring into my plate like it was my grave.

I ripped off my Spicer hat and apron and slunk through the store to where I could get a peek out the front window and see this Mr. Dexter.

"Mr. Christmas!" The voice of Mrs. Spicer sung out

beside me. "I have need of a new tea cozy," she says, and I am ashamed to admit that I said:

"Go to hay, ma'am. I'm busy right now."

Well, her and her moustache sure bristled at that. Just then the man in gray walked out into the street, and I left Mrs. Spicer to stew. I slipped out the store and followed him, but didn't have to go far, for he crossed right over to the Hill Hotel, and a coupla minutes later I saw him pacing back and forth in a second-floor window.

Though I had probly been fired already, I snuck back in the Emporium's back door. In the storeroom I found paper and pen and in the dark I wrote this note in a backwards hand to disguize my self:

> I know who you are and what you did. Meet me at the triple cactus today at sundown.
>
> Your Own Worst Enemy

I stuck it in a envelope and wrote, "Mr. Dexter, Hill Hotel, <u>URGINT</u>" on it.

"Billy," somebody said, and I jumped so hard my hand smeared the page. It was Amy, one of my fellow clarks. "Mr. Spicer's looking for you," she said, "and he's barking like a dog."

"Fat cur," I said, "let him." My morals, as you can

see, was on the downslide. "Amy, do you want to earn 2 bits?"

"2 bits!" she said. That was a whole day's wages for a Spicer clark, so Amy musta figgered whatever I was asking for, it couldn't be moral nor ethical nor right. "Sure," she said.

"Go over and hand this letter at the hotel, but don't say where you got it. Anybody asks, just say a man give it to you."

"Money first," Amy said, like a true citizen of Hill. I paid her the 2 bits. "For a extra nickel," she said, "I'll let you kiss me."

"Maybe another time," I said. "Run."

I spied in the street from behind a buggy whilst Amy passed the envelope to the hotel clerk in the eyeshade. I saw how he headed up the stairs with it and how Mr. Dexter in that second-floor window turned around a minute later like he had heard a knock. He left the window and come back with my letter in his hand. He stared at the handwriting on the front and looked quizzicle, then ripped it open and read, real still. He stood the longest while staring at that page. Then he bruptly looked down into the street almost as if he felt somebody watching him. I ducked back behind the buggy. When I looked again, he was gone. A minute later he walked out the hotel and headed fast up the street towards Grady's stable. The dove-gray suit bulged at the hips where he was wearing a brace of pistols.

The triple cactus where I asked him to meet me was a landmark outside of town, and it'd take him till sunset to get there. Sometime between here and his return, I had to get into his room and snoop for some truth.

Suzi Generous was leaning at the Golden Eagle bar right where I expected her, with her shape on display like a theayter markee.

"Hey, cowboy," she said. "I told you you shoulda wrote me that letter."

"Get outa here, boy," Fly said from behind the bar. I felt flattered to be the kinda person one would kick out of a saloon. That takes some character.

"Suzi," I said, "you want to earn a easy dollar?"

"Senator's in town?" she said.

"No," I said, "I want you to walk me up into the Hill Hotel and slip out down the back stairs."

"Is this strickly legal?" she said.

"It sure is not."

"Money first," she said, just like Amy, and I have no doubt that she and Amy are fee-male colleegs today. I give her the dollar in small change which she slipped down her front and she give me her arm like a childhood sweetheart. The snuggle of her clinking bosoms as we went up the street was practicly worth the dollar.

Inside the hotel lobby the clerk in the black eye-shade was pigeonholing mail like a condemned prisoner. Suzi said, "Anybody asks for me—"

"Number 33," says the clerk without even turning.

Suzi led me up the stairs of my previous downfall. At the second-floor landing she winked to me and tiptoed off towards the back stairs and disappeared. I found the room I wanted and then bruptly realized I did not have a key. Right on the other side of that door was inlightenment, if only I could get to it.

"Can I help you, sir?" asked a voice.

It was that homely maid who showered cigar butts on my head my first day in Hill. She smiled real sweet at me again now and was transformed into a beauty, despite of her missing teeth.

"Mr. Dexter," I said, "he sent me up here to get his gray gloves, now I clean forgot his key."

"I have a key," she said. She took the great metal key ring off her belt and opened the door for me like a dream.

"Thank you," I said, "aren't you a godsend," and all at once I felt sorry for the shabbyness of her life and the goodness of her heart. Women sure had been greasing my way towards inlightenment that day, but I have found that that is true of life as a hole. Women mostly all carry the keys to wisdom around with them. Women and Injuns. Men are in the mainly just fools.

"My name is Charity, in case you need me," she said, and I know my mother coulda spun a parabull outa her name for days. "You're real welcome, sir."

She give me one more radiant smile and I could have dropped on my knees and married her there, but I had other business. She went off to shower cigar butts on the heads of traveling sinners, and I slippt into Mr. Dexter's room. I had to tiptoe real quiet, for it lay dreckly over the front desk. If that clerk heard me, he'd come right up.

The place looked as if this Dexter was living there, by the mount of luggage and effects scattered about. The first thing struck my eyes was all the guns, a small armery of pistols and rifles and a barbed whip that made my ribs cry out, for it had once ripped the skin off my back in a royo. Next was some ashes still smoking in a ashtray on the bureau. A piece of unburnt paper sat amidst the ashes, and on it I read the word *"URGINT"* in my hand. Dexter had burnt the evidence. Last was something else I reckonized with a start: Romulus's letter to Jenny propped up on the dresser but practicly un-reckonizable, for it was scrawled all over in some other hand with the foulest obseenities. I'd perfer not to numerate them. I'd perfer not to have even seen them. They was pure hatred. They was madness.

A footstep caught my ear. Somebody was creeping about in the corridor outside—and they was creeping my way. The doorknob rattled as a hand outside fumbled it. I concockted a million lies, not one of them any good. Then the door opened and Romulus Vollmer stood there looking at me.

"Rom!" I cried out, and he motioned for me to be still. He looked behind him and stepped in and eased the door shut.

"Scrib," he whispered, and looked me up and down as if he had never seen me before. "Jesus, Scrib, you're alive!" And he threw his arms about me. "Where have you been?"

"Well," I said, "mostly at Spicer's Emporeeum, degrading my self into a base wage slave."

"Say, what happened to your face?" he said, and for the first time I answered the question truthfully.

I said, "I met up with the man who lives in this room. That's what happened."

"He's the one set the Triple X afire," said Rom. He

rapidly explained how he laid waiting all the night after the blaze and in the morning had trailed Dexter but had lost him, then found him again here in Hill.

"It ain't easy watching him," Rom whispered. "He disappears from time to time during the night, and sometimes he'll be gone for days. Then out in the street today I saw you watching him and I followed you in here. Who is this person and what's he after?"

I was about to tell my side of things when something through the window caught his eye and Rom said: "He's coming back."

I looked out and saw Dexter in the street right below us, with Sheriff Ackelberg alongside him. Just then Dexter pointed up right at the window Rom and me was standing in, in full view.

Rom said, "Follow me," and all was a chaos for a minute. Rom dashed for the door, but the desk clerk was right on the other side, coming in. Rom stiff-shouldered him out of his way, but the clerk grabbed me as I was going by and held on tight. Rom tried beating him off, but the clerk kept me gripped by the fabric of my sleeve, then Ackelberg and Dexter come rounding the stairs onto the landing.

"Run, Rom," I said, and he took off down the corridor the other way and leept out a open window and was gone. Then the corridor was filled with people.

"Sheriff," Dexter said, "arrest this thief."

First day I rode into Hill the Sheriff told me he had room at the jail for me. Now he marched me across the street and proved it.

"You been trying hard enough to get in," he said as he locked me in my cell. "Now you're here. For a *brief* while, anyhow." He grinned, and his silver toothpick glinted. For in the city of Hill, where all goods is sacred, thiefery was a hanging offense.

Chapter Twelve

WHILST IN CAPTIVITY, I MEET A HYENA, THE MAN IN THE BLACK HAT, AND A VISITER FROM AFAR

T he Hill jail vyed with the Hill Hotel for comfort, cept the rats wasn't as well fed and the jail smellt better. It give off a roma of clammyness and cold stone and the pails that passed for toilets. For food, you got slop three times a day. For company, you enjoyed several breeds of lice, all of them a shade too friendly.

Upon arrival I stood at my cell door and screamed till I was chartroose that I didn't belong there, but my voice was drowned out by all the other chartroose-faced folks screaming the same thing. Who was I to cry to anyhow, when Sheriff Ackelberg was wearing my own stolen boots? I climbed up on my cot and proclaimed my inner-cence out the bars of my window, but all I attracted was the notice of Suzi Generous, who was passing in the street with some unfortunate soon-to-be-robbed cus-tomer on her arm. She heard my cry and called back, "I *told* you you shoulda wrote me that letter!" After that I avoided the window, if the streets was full of moralists like Suzi Generous preaching at me.

Well, I had reached bottom and acted accordionly, sighing on my cot and wishing I had never fled the white picket fences of Saint Louis. I did not know if Romulus had escaped, or even if he was dead or alive.

My second day I had a visiter. Just after morning slop, the Sheriff led in a ferrety-faced, noisy woman with red nails and a voice like a vice and more teeth than I ever seen on a human being.

"Mr. Christmas," she said, "I'm Harleen Trendley, chief critic of *Entertainment Hourly*. What an absolute honor to meet you. Why, I'm giddy, Mr. Christmas! Positively *giddy!*"

She was so giddy she reached her hand through the bars and gripped my arm, and her nails sliced up my shirt. Now I knew why she was known as Harleen "The Hyena" Trendley.

"*May* I touch," she said, "the town's most-talked-about criminal?"

"I'm not a criminal," I said. "I'm a innercent."

She trilled out a laugh and took out a leopard-skin notebook complete with claws.

"Your trial," she said, "is going to be this season's four-star, all-thumbs-up, A-plus-plus entertainment sensation. I've got my review half written already. 'A real crowd-lassooer!' 'Get out your kerchiefs!' 'Ten-gallon fun!' 'Gallop, don't trot to see it!' May I quote you?" she said suddenly.

I said, "I haven't said anything."

"So," she said, "how does it feel to be about to be condemned? Are you *thrilled*?"

This was when I lost control and made a coarse suggestion, which she took a fence at. I don't need to specify what I suggested. Many of us have suggested it to folks in our times. I hang my head to think of it now. Anyway, Harleen Trendley upped and left, and I doubted my trial would get a A++ anymore, though my hanging might.

That was the same day I got a cellmate. Sometime after midday slop the Sheriff unlocked my cell door and thrust in a man who tumbled onto the cot across from mine. He was a black man of some age and he was wearing, to my intreeg, a black hat with a bright blue band round the crown.

"Welcome to Hill—*boy*," the Sheriff said, and went off to polish his toothpick. The new man spit in the cell bucket for answer and stripped off his hat to reveal a busted nose and a beat-up face, which he rubbed all over with the palm of his hand as if he was washing it, like a cat.

"Who are you," I said, "and what are you doing in here?"

"My name is Tazwell Turner," he proclaimed, "and I'm in here for doing *nothing*, that's what." The man's eyes blazed. "I was standing on the street and that b——d Sheriff tells me to move on. I told him where *he* could move to, and he arrests me as a vagrant. I'm in this jail for being black, that's what I'm in here for."

"Have I ever seen you before?" I said.

"I doubt it," he said. He was still a-fire with his anger and barely paying me any mind.

I said, "I think you're looking for me."

That caught his ear. "What?" he said. "Looking for you?"

I said, "My name is William Stanley Christmas."

He stared at me in a mazement and then he said,

"Son, I been searching all over creation for you!"

"I fled you for a time," I said. "I thought you was trying to kill me."

"Kill you?" he said, and he laughed. "I *got* something for you." And he reaches in his shirt pocket and takes out a battered and smudged-up envelope and holds it out to me. Even in the twilight of that cell I could see that under all the batter and smudge that envelope was a familyar shade of lavender. On its front was written "For William Stanley Christmas" in lavender ink, in a bold and flowry hand that I reckonized well. That envelope had journeyed a long ways to get to me.

I stared at the thing and bruptly realized that though I was a letter writer, I had never in my life received a letter of my own, addressed solely to me, until that very second.

"It's your message," Mr. Turner says. "Are you gonna take it or not?"

I took the envelope, and in my shaking hand it fluttered like a divining rod that has found deep deep water. Now I too stood before that invisible door that comes with all messages and which I had stood porter at for so many other people. *A letter comes*, I thought, *you gotta open it and read. That's life, Scrib.*

So I slippt my finger under the flap and gently

unstuck the fradjle glue. As I opened it, the envelope breathed out some ancient lavender which filled up the cell. Inside it I found just one small sheet of notepaper, dated three years before, some days after I left Saint Louis.

April 27, 1860

My dear son,

Please come talk to me sometime. Forgive me.

All love,
Mother

That was all, and when I had read it I bust into tears like a child and pressed that hard page to my eyes as if it was the softest kerchief. The stench of the lavender only made things worse. Tazwell lay on his cot and left me to my self by whistling softly as if he wasn't aware of my weeping, though I coulda swore his eyes filled up too, for he dabbed at them quietly once or twice. I felt I had gained my mother again only in time to lose her forever, and I sighed accordionly. If she could have seen me there in that jail cell, it would have killt her.

"What do I owe you for this, Mr. Turner?" I finally

said, and he said, "Not a thing. It's all paid for."

"But are you sure that I don't know you somehow?"

"I don't see how you could," he said.

"What are you," I said, "and where are you from, and how did you come by this letter?"

Being so interested in him, I almost forgot I was to be condemned to the rope not one day hence.

"I'm a letter writer," he said, "and I come from Chicago Illinois. My family has never been slaves, always free—merchants and businesspeople, and we always lived without trouble from white folks or any other kind. But I never liked the city, and I didn't want to sit in a shop all day all the rest of my life. So in the spring of the year eighteen hundred and thirty-seven, age of fifteen, I left my home and started moving westwards."

I almost said, "I run away too," but let it go.

"I was always a good scholar," he said, "and I always had a fine clear hand."

"Me too," I did say aloud.

"So I decided I would set up as a letter writer for Negroes. I would pass on good news and bad news for those who could not, and I would have my freedom, too. I also enjoy the differences of the people I meet. For folks sure can be various."

"Why," I said, "I say that myself all the time!"

"I did leave letter writing for dissipation for a time," he said. "Whiskey and hoors and tobacco and gaming."

"I tried that too," I said, "for a couple hours."

"Wasn't to my taste," he said, and I said, "Not to mine neither. Plus I lost my belt and shoes and 13 dollars and 13 cents."

"The long in short of it is," he said, "I come back to letter writing. Problem was, I had lived without trouble for so long, I didn't know the trouble being a black man could be in parts of this world. And I started running into plenty of trouble. Seven times I been wrongfully in jail and once I got smeared with boiling tar and barely escaped with my life. Then in Saint Louis Missouri I was delivering a letter and got mistook for a runaway slave—"

"Wait a minute," I said. "Did you hide in the river, mongst the reeds?"

"I did," he said.

"Did they find you and tie you up to four ropes and drag you through the street?"

"They did," he said. "How did you know that?'

"Because I do know you," I said. "I saw you that night, and I can see you still. Staring at me through a window whilst I sat at my table syphering. We have looked in our eyes once before."

"Well, well," he said. "Well, well. How are people and things not connected up."

I said, "I thought they was going to hang you."

"I thought so too," he said. "And I woulda *been* hanged, but for your mother."

"My mother?" says I.

"Well," he said, "she *is* part of the Network."

"Network," I said. "What Network?"

"The Railroad," he said. "She helps black folks to safety all the time."

"No," I said.

"God's truth," he said, and held up his hand to swear it. "She got me out of jail. She set me on my way. But first she asked of me a favor."

"This letter," I said, which was still in my hand.

"That letter," he said. "I wanted to get farther west anyhow—as far out of trouble as I could get. And I owed her deeply. So the little favor turned into a long one. About three years long."

"You didn't go east first, looking for me?" I said.

"Why?" he said. "Because you *told* her you were going east? Your mother saw straight through that. She said to me, 'Tazwell, he'll go west, you just find the most foolish place he could go to and he'll be there.'"

"And here I am," I said.

I reflected a moment how you cannot say anything simple or sure about this world, for everything has a doubleness to it, and a mystery, a secret life hidden underneath the one we see like a underground river. A wanted criminal can be nothing but a walleyed man named Duane from a farm in Tennessee. A lavendered schoolteacher may be a worker for the Underground Railroad Network. A sheriff might be a criminal and a minister a secret drunker and a repyootable storekeeper a seller of dirty pictures. There was reasons for all this somewhere but they was part of the mystery and doubleness of life. I only wished I could live longer enough to investigate it.

"Now you got my end of things," said Tazwell Turner, "what the h—l are *you* doing in here?"

I told him my tale from the top and he got pergressively troubled. Several times he washed his face with the palm of his hand as he listened, as if to wipe away all that he was hearing.

"It's bad," he said when I had finished, for his troubles had made him into a truth-teller.

"Real bad," I said, for I was turning into a realist real fast. "We two sure know how to stay in trouble, don't we."

"I'm about to head my self into more trouble," he said. "Soon as they let me out of here, I'm going back east, to the War. I used to say I didn't have a dog in that fight."

I said, "I used to say that too."

"I used to say I wasn't a part of any Union, that I was a free being," he said. "But I see now I'm a part of a real big Union whether I like it or not. A Union that's bigger than the United States of America. And I got a dog in that fight, all right. That dog is me."

I was no safer from the rope than I had been that morning, but somehow I felt better to have Tazwell there with me. And so we talked till dawn and become acquainted on what was to be the final night of my life. From time to time, a great fear of death would come upon me and I would begin to tremble, but Tazwell always brought me back to peace.

Next morning after slop the Sheriff come to fetch me to trial. A deputy cuffed my wrists behind me whilst the Sheriff waggled a gun at me and gnawed his silver toothpick. I don't know if you ever had a gun pointed at you, but it ain't so carefree as in the melodraymas. Lighthearted banter don't atchley spring to mind, and you feel like your guts are gonna drop out of you all in one piece. Before we was separated, Tazwell gripped my hand hard and said, "Don't despair," though to my ears it sounded awful like, "Nice knowing you, brother."

All I took with me was the lavender letter, buttoned up in my shirt pocket like an amlet. I had little need of anything. It was to be my last day on earth.

Chapter Thirteen

I COME TO JUDGMENT

A great crowd observed as I got paraded to the courthouse in City Hall. All the way down Main Street, I remembered how Tazwell had been driven like a animal through the streets of Saint Louis, and how he had stumbled against a fence and I had looked in his eyes. I wondered if any boy in Hill was looking out his window that day and getting led to ponder about life and justice. I did notice boys throughout the crowd peddling copies of *Entertainment Hourly*, which bore my face on the cover looking badly drawn, but downright devlish. Outside City Hall, scalpers was selling tickets to my trial at inflatable prices. And I saw posters stuck up everplace that said, "Come to a

Public Hanging! Free Admission!"

City Hall sat atop the spine of a major geographical fault, and as we ascended the steps towards the doors the whole building tipped as if to swallow us. Above the lintel, written in stone, was the words "Vanity, vanity, all is vanity"—a curious motto for a town dedicated to entertainment, restaurants and shopping.

The courtroom swarmed full up to busting, and through the tall windows you could see grown people sitting on each other's shoulders outside, trying to get a gander. The room was sloped like a ramp because of the fault underneath it, so the balances on the statue of Justice up front was wildly a-tilt.

Still in handcuffs I got shoved to a table and met my lawyer, a man named Johnson, I believe, who had one arm and was very drunk. In the courtroom pews I saw the Spicers dressed as for church and Suzi Generous eating cotton candy and all my fellow clarks from the Emporium and Fly the barkeep and Harleen Trendley sitting on a aisle with that leopard-skin notebook, writing her review of my trial before it even happened. I didn't see Rom nor Dexter anyplace. The crowd was shoulder-to-shoulder, yet I had never in my life felt so alone.

"All rise for the master of ceremonies!" somebody announced. "Judge Oliver McGuinness!"

The audience pushed to its feet, which caused the floor of the whole courtroom to shift and tilt, and the pans of Justice swung the other way and banged like pie tins calling people to lunch. Oliver McGuinness marched in wearing black velveety robes with a bootaneer, for he was chief judge in Hill as well as mayor, though it seemed a conflict of disinterest. He took a bow and kissed his fingers to his fans, who applauded voiciferously.

"Set," the announcer said, like a dog trainer, and everbody set. The courtroom tilted back and Justice banged her tins all over again.

"The People of Hill versus William Stanley Christmas, alias Scrib," the announcer proclaimed. "The charge is thiefery, and may God have mercy on his rotten dirty soul."

"Who brings this charge?" the judge asked like he didn't know already.

"Mr. Edward Dexter," the announcer said.

"A fine gentleman," the judge said, "known throughout our town. As for the accused," he said, "I happen to know the young man." He fixed a eye on me. The question markers of his moustache was waxed up stiffly and cast all kinds of doubt on my chances of living. "He's a young libertine. A no-good scamp, dedicated to personal pollution. That said," he said, "how does he plead?"

"Guilty," said my lawyer.

"Wait a minute," I said.

The judge ignored me. "Let's talk about sentencing," he said, "and see if he's old enough to hang."

The audience cheered as one.

"Wait a minute," I said.

"Hang him now!" somebody called from the crowd. It sounded like the mail-sorter in the black eyeshade. The Judge banged his gabble for silence and said, "All in good time. Don't you realize the show trial must go on?"

"Your Honor," said a man, who I guessed was the persecuting attorney. "I have evidence relating to this boy's rotten character."

"Wait a minute," I said again.

His Honor banged his gabble and said, "Sit down, boy, or I'll have you restrained."

"I'm restrained already," I said, and my drunken lawyer pulled me down into my chair and fell back asleep.

The persecutor said, "Your Honor, some papers was found in the boy's room which I believe are pertnent to the severity of his punishment."

He held up the papers I had written in my broom closet late at nights.

He said, "This boy, I submit, is a spy who has snooped upon and villafied and tradooced the citizens of this fair city. I select some samples at random."

He took up a page and read a pertickly de-taled description of the Spicer women's eating habits and a hourlong conversation they had about whether corn frit-ters tasted better than potato fritters.

"This is slander!" cried the Spicers behind me.

The crowd laughed, but as the persecutor read more and more pages about more and more citizens, the laughter changed. He read how Mr. Dawson the bank president come into the Emporium ever other day to buy dirty pictures and how much sour-mash whiskey Reverend Bunce consumed. He read how Mayor McGuinness told me the purpose of life was Senshal Intoxication and how the Sheriff stole my boots in cahoots with Suzi Generous. Some people was edified, some was amused, some listened in shamed silents, but just about everbody got insulted one way or another. By the end of it the whole room was screaming, "Hang him, hang him!"

"Your Honor," the persecutor summed up, "I don't care how old this boy is. I say he oughta swing!"

Judge McGuinness said, "So be it. The only

question"—as if he didn't already know the answer—"is when."

The mob was already on its feet shouting *"Now! Hang him now!* String him up!" My lawyer remained deep asleep through all this racket, blowing bubbles like a sucking babe, and ever time I rose to speak, the Sheriff tugged me down by the handcuffs.

Judge McGuinness banged his gabble to quiet the hubbub and said, "Very well, ladies and gentlemen. It's the voice of the people. Take that scum away and do what you will. I wash my hands of him."

Now I felt myself grabbed from behind to be carried outside to the only sizable tree in Hill, which had but one sizable purpose, which was hangings.

This was when a crash stopped everthing, as one of them tall windows up the wall exploded into a thousand shivers. Now I have said that life is not like a melodrayma—but it would not be life if it didn't suprize us ever now and again. For at that moment, through the exploding window, a horse comes flying into the room with a cloaked rider, and makes a perfect four-hoof landing right before the judge's bench. Men, women, and children screamed as the mystery rider loosed off some blasts from a pair of pepperbox pistols, then unfolded him self to reveal who but Crazy James Kincaid, looking pertickly crazed.

"Hold it right there!" he cried. "Don't nobody move!"

Duane's hair was standing straight up on his head in more than the usual mazement, and his wall eyes was flopping about the room every which ways. Not a person there but thought he was eyeing them. He must have been wearing six bandoleros full of catridges strapped over his chest and had about fifty pistols holstered about his body.

"It's Crazy James . . . !" people was whispering. "Crazy James Kincaid . . . !"

A couple more shots quieted them.

"My boys are covering the front and the back, so don't nobody try anything funny," Duane cried. "They got Gatling guns and they'll gattle the whole lot of you. So put yer hands up! Everbody!"

Hands shot up like a schoolroom full of smart kids. The hands holding me behind let me go.

"Drop that gun, Sheriff!" another voice cried out, and now Romulus leept onto a chair with a gun out. "Drop it, or I'll blow off your hand!"

I heard Ackelberg's pistol clang to the floor behind me. Duane was staring at Romulus like he didn't know who the hay this new person was, but it didn't matter. Rom was now part of the Kincaid Gang.

"Didn't I tell you I had you all covered?" Duane cried. "Now this innercent boy here," he said of me, "is under my protection. Unleash him, Sheriff."

My hands got grasped behind for a moment as my cuffs were unlocked, and then my wrists went free.

"Hop on," Duane said to me, and I leept up behind him on Esmeralda. "Don't nobody try to follow me, or I'll sink this town farther than she's sunk already! Them's the words of Crazy James Kincaid. And don't forget—I ain't just walleyed. *I'm crazy!*"

Now this was superior drayma for the entertainment-hungry citizens of Hill, and was met by a mediate round of wild applause. I spotted Harleen Trendley thrusting her spotted notebook towards Duane and wailing for his autograph. I knew we'd get five stars yet.

Duane yelled, "I'M COMIN' OUT NOW, BOYS!" and the crowd parted and the room tipped the other way and Justice and her pie tins toppled right off their pedestal as me and Duane galloped down the aisle of the courtroom, through the front doors, and flew over the stairs straight onto Main Street. About a hunderd pistols went off in City Hall behind us, and Duane said to me, "Hang on tight."

Esmeralda reared up pictureskly, then we charged up Main Street with Duane firing blind over both our shoulders. I nearly flew off Esmeralda a few times, for she was hurtling the sinkholes like a champion.

"Didn't I tell you she was a steeplechaser?" Duane cried to me. Duane sure seemed more than just walleyed at that moment. He seemed truly, atchley crazy. I hardly cared, being happy to have my neck still jointed to my shoulders.

"How did you know how to find me?" I yelled.

He yelled back, "I looked you up in *Entertainment Hourly!*"

As we approached the P.O., Frank the Postmaster comes running out into the street with that mail sack in his hand.

"Hey, Scrib!" he cried. "Scrib! I still got all this mail for you!"

"Thanks, Postmaster!" I cried, and as we flew by I grabbed the sack right out his hand.

Duane pulled up at Grady's, and in a trice I was cradled on Gabe. Not five minutes later we was out of the sinkholes of Hill and back in the flat of the scrub. You could hear the commotion back in Hill for a time, then the echoes faded like the dreaming stones of the

Talking Rocks. Duane slowed us down to a trot.

"They're going to trail us," I said.

"I have eluded my trailers for many years," Duane said. "'Elusion' is my middle name. But I see you have not taken my advice."

"Advice?" I said.

"Your hair, Scrib," he said. "You have not aerated your *brain*."

For a letter writer, you sure could not say my life lacked adventure.

Chapter Fourteen

IN WHICH I REGAIN SOMETHING I HAD LOST

We arrived at Duane's hideaway amongst the Talking Rocks just after nightfall. I fell right off to sleep and dropped into dreams so full of hanging I'm suprized I didn't wake with rope burn round my neck. The smell of morning coffee roused me, but Duane was nowhere to be seen when I awoke, though Esmeralda and Jupiter was there. So I poured myself a cup of Crazy James's gut-cleansing brew and sat down at the mouth of the cave and I pondered.

Here's where I started: I had got away for now, but people was going to be after me. I had been pursued before and tried to flee, but that had not worked. My only allturnative was to get to the bottom of all this and clear my name. Now much of what had happened was a mystery, but I knew as sure as Shakespeare that it was Rom's love letter to Jenny that incited Dexter to attack me. This meant that Jenny Smeed sat at the middle of a circle of evil. One would have to be a fool to enter that circle, but I had proved my self a fool time and time again by now and seemed cut out for the job.

After coffee I found my way back down into the gulch that Duane had drug me out of half-dead. I could see the tracks of the pallet he pulled me on, fresh as yesterday. I come upon some of my dried blood, sprayed over the rubble. I even found the bloody tooth I had spit out, laying on a rock, picked clean and polished by ants. But that was not what I was looking for—I was after something I half-guessed might still be there.

I found it, too, under a rock where Dexter had tossed it, not a dozen yards from where he ambushed me. It was my writing bag, with paper and pens and letters and the ink bottles miraculously unbroke. Sure enough, there was Duane's letter to his family and Pierre's letter to the President and Mrs. Clarence Witherspoon's letter asking Oxferd if life was but a dream. All the envelopes was there cept the one Dexter had taken—Romulus's love letter to Jenny.

As I come back to the cave, Duane was sitting at the mouth and jumped to his feet when he saw what was slung over my shoulder.

"Don't tell me," he said.

"It's the letter bag," I said. "With your letter to your folks and everthing."

"Scrib," he said, "you sure do have a gift for drayma."

I tossed the bag down next to the mail sack I took from Frank the Postmaster.

I said, "People are going to be after me," and Duane said, "That they will. But it's normal."

"My Injun friend Pierre," I said, "he says somebody's always after everybody."

"He must be a wise Injun," Duane said, "to come up with something as murky as that."

I said, "I'd be happy to go on the road with you as a fugitive."

"I appreciate that offer, Scrib," he said. "But I don't think fugitivity is your true calling."

I said, "Then I think I'm gonna head back east."

Now this was a out-and-out lie. I didn't want to tell him what I atchley planned, for what I intended was dangerous, and he might try to talk me out of it or offer to help me. I did not want to ask more of Duane than he had done already.

"I better disappear good and solid my self for a while," he said, "having made a suprize guest appearance at your hanging. Think I'll elude upland for a time, to the Elusion Fields. But I'm gonna miss your company," he said.

I said, "I never did thank you for saving my neck a whole second time."

"I will tell you how you can thank me," Duane said. "You can write a post-cryptum on my letter. I got something to add."

I joyed at the chance to dip my pen, and right then and there I spread out my papers and my tools just as of old and got ready to take his dictation. Duane frowned in silents a minute, assembling his thoughts.

"'P.S.,'" he finally said. "'It's some days later and I'm still fine.'" He stopped. "Okay," he said. "That's all."

"That's all?" I said.

"I thought they'd want to know."

"I can write in whatever you want. Pages and pages."

"Naw," he said. "I think that's everthing."

"Okay," I said. I had started saying "okay" again. I read that as a good sign.

I took my leave of Duane that same day. Gabe was all packed up, and by the eager twitchy look of him he knew we was headed back on the circuit. Duane had one final advice on hair-style before we parted.

"Keep in mind," he said, "that 'air' and 'hair' rhyme together. And don't think it ain't on purpose. Nothing ain't on purpose."

Then he give me a bottle of his stomach settler as a going-away gift, which it turned out really was stomach settler. I got up on Gabe and rode off. A minute later, Duane and his amazed hair was fading out of sight behind some rocks. When he was gone, I did hear his voice cry out one last time, as if he was one of the Talking Rocks:

"Don't forget to aerate your brain!"

That same night, laying out in the scrub unable to sleep and listening to the *chirp chirp chirp* of bats overhead, I looked up and saw a moondog, a slice of rainbow in the nighttime sky bright as a cut of watermelon, and the moon was haloed by a hazy silver ring. It is a beautiful but ghostly thing to see a rainbow at night. But the Injuns know what a moondog stands for. Pierre had told me.

That moondog meant bad weather.

Chapter Fifteen

ANOTHER MURDER

Mongst the letters in the mail sack was a few addressed to Nell and Robert Pollack, and as the Pollack ranch lay right in my path, I decided to drop the letters on my way, little suspecting what I'd meet there.

The Pollacks was the sort of folks that seem to naturally know something important about life, the sort you hang about so you can find it out too. Half the clothes I wore was passed on to me by the Pollacks, and the blanket I slept on ever night was a Pollack blanket. They was good plain people, with a spread of land as big and open as their hearts. If they had been letterate, who knows what they could have been in the world. "Maybe I'll learn letters after I die, Scrib," Nell Pollack once said to me. "For Heaven will be chock full of time." She said it as simply as she believed it. She was the kind of person that if she tossed God or Heaven into a conversation, you wasn't even embarrassed.

The Pollacks often had a compliment of family or friends staying at their house, so I was suprized when I saw no wagons or buggies drawn up out front. As I got closer, I heard no voices raised in talk or laughter from inside, and again I wondered, for the Pollack house was rarely quiet.

The house felt like a funeral. Nobody greeted me, like they usually did. Food and drink was spoiling on a sideboard, feeding flies, for nobody was there to touch it.

I walked through to the ranch's office and found Robert Pollack Junior sitting slumped at the old desk where his father always sat. When he looked up, I knew that only Death could have hollowed and extinguished his eyes like that. My heart sunk to meet whatever had happened.

"Robert," I said, "what is all this?"

He said: "Somebody has killt Ma and Pa."

"Killt them," I said.

"Late night yesterday," he said.

"Where," I said. "How."

"Right here," he said, and he nodded to the very room we was in. "Cleaned out the safe and run. You know your self that safe was always open."

I could see the safe right there behind the desk, its door gaping open still and its insides empty. I stood stupidly looking at the letters I had brought for his parents, clutched in my numb hand.

"Whoever it was, he clubbed Pa in the head," he said. "Then he whipped him—whipped him even after he was dead."

"Whipped him . . . ," I said.

"Guess Ma musta heard something and walked in. He killt her the same way. I found the two of 'em my self," he said, "right there on the floor. Battered till you wouldn't even've known 'em. God d——n it," he bust out with. "God d——n it!"

"Who did this," I said.

Robert Junior said, "They think it's Kincaid."

I was about to say something, but he fixed his eyes on me hard and bore into me.

"I hear Kincaid is a friend of yours. I heard about your trial for thiefery and how he saved you. I found this on the floor here," Robert Junior said, and dug in his pocket and laid something on the desk. "This belong to your friend Kincaid?" It was a gray cloth-covered button—and could have come off the vest of a hand-made dove-gray suit.

"Robert," I said, "I'm not a thief."

"Ackelberg's looking for you already," Robert said. "There's Wanted posters out with your name on them."

I said, "Robert, I *know* it wasn't Kincaid who did this."

"Okay," he said, "then who?"

"Same person who whipped and clubbed me till I was nearly dead. A man called Edward Dexter."

But he wasn't listening.

"I'd kill you right now," he said through his teeth. "You or anybody else. If Ackelberg sees you, he'll shoot you without asking first. Now get the h——l out this house."

Them letters in my hand felt like they weight fifty pounds. "Mr. Robert Pollack, Care of Scrib. Mrs. Nell Pollack, Care of Scrib." I thought to myself, *The Pollacks was in my care, and now they're dead.* I laid the envelopes on the desk, for what else could I do but deliver them? Then I left, and when I had gone out of the room I heard Robert Junior weeping behind me.

Gabe was suprized when I come back out so fast and remounted. Usually we took our ease at the Pollack ranch. Instead, we rode back out the gate and into the dark. For tonight Gabe and I would rest, as well as we could, in the open, I with my head uneasy on a Pollack blanket, while Nell and Robert Pollack enjoyed Heaven's charity and a eternity chock full of time. Well, they had breathed their spirit into the world. Now it would have its effect.

Middle of the night, I was wakened by thunder, and soon after that the rain started to fall. The moondog had predicted aptly. The monsoons was arriving.

Chapter Sixteen

I DELIVER A STONISHING MESSAGE AND GO TO THE SMEEDS, WHERE I MEET DEXTER

By morning the rain turned the scrub to sludge. I slithered up the mudslides to the top of Demon Butte, but Pierre was gone and the place deserted. His firesite was a puddle of ashes and the reeds of his wickiup was scattered over the ground, which meant he had been kicked off and forced to move again. I knew Pierre wouldn't go away without leaving a message of some kind, and I found his note at the edge of the drop: two sticks stuck in the ground and crossed to make a V, with a pointed stick laid in the crotch pointing like a needle north-north-west towards Candle Mesa. You don't always need ink and pen to write a note.

Sure enough, Pierre was camped under a overhang

at the foot of Candle Mesa, right where the needle had pointed me. He didn't show any more suprize than usual when I arrived, just watched me dismount like I was a lizard that had scuttled cross his view. Meanwhile I could hardly contain myself, though I tried not to show it, for I was carrying something rare and wonderful— something so rich even I could not imagine it. And for once I hoped to see some suprize on Pierre's stony face.

"I brought you something, Pierre," I said.

"Yuh-huh," he said, and spit in the fire as if to say, What could you bring me I'd ever want.

"It's a letter from Washington, D.C.," I said, "and it's addressed to you."

My hopes was not in vain, for I saw on Pierre's face what probly passes for suprize the whole human world over.

"You expecting a letter?" I said. "From someplace called, what was it now? *The White House?* Guess we better see what's in it," I said, and I ambled as slow as I could over to Gabe. I laid out my things to dry and I wiped my face and hands with a towel and hung up my poncho and finally unstrapped my writing bag and brung it over to the fire.

"Now where did I put that letter," I said. "This it?" No, that's not it. . . . Is this it? No, that's not it. . . ."

"Go to h——l," Pierre said. Now he thought I was joshuing.

"Here it is," I said, and drew out a small white envelope on creamy bond paper probly worth $10.00 a ream. This was the important letter Frank the Postmaster had been thrusting at me for weeks, and I was too much of a horse's pasterior to take.

I pointed to the upper corner. "See right there?" I said. "That says 'The White House, Washington, D.C.'" He squinched at the printing on the envelope.

I said, "Down here, this handwriting says, 'To Mr. Pierre Trakki, Care of Scrib, Hill Post Office, Hill City District.' Should I unstick?" He made a motion that I took to be a yes. I fumbled my knife out of its sheath and slit the envelope as neat as I could. My own heart pounded like a beaten rug as I took out the page.

"'Office of the President of the United States,'" I read. "Here's a seal of office at the top, showing that it's real."

I showed that to Pierre.

"Now here's the note," I said, and read the handwriting, but my voice was shaking so bad I had to clear my throat and start again. 'August 5, 1863. Dear Mr. Trakki. I have received all your letters and read them. Forgive me that the prosecution of the War has delayed my answer. Your anger and sorrow, sir, are justified. When this awful struggle for Union has been resolved I shall do all in my power to bring your people the justice you so eloquently call for, and to return to them their lands. Today I have spoken with my Interior Secretary on this matter. Suffering will see righteousness. Until that day, sir, I remain, Abraham Lincoln.'"

There it was at the bottom. Not "Abraham Lincoln, President," or "President Abraham Lincoln," just "Abraham Lincoln," like he was not greater than we were, but simply another person on the face of the earth.

I handed the page to Pierre, and the envelope. He looked from one to the other in a kind of mazement.

"Read it again," Pierre said, and I read the letter through twice more. Then while rain dripped from the overhang, we sat in the dry and pondered in silents together. After Pierre had pondered sufficient, he folded up the letter and envelope and wrapped them in a piece of deerskin and tied that round his neck like a charm. Then he roasted a coupla ground squirrels over the fire and we ate and pondered some more. It is a awesome thing to be sitting on the hard ground eating toasted squirrel while feeling directly threaded up to the great and mighty. It was as if a rope had been let down from the sky and touched us on the shoulder.

Next morning I outlined my fix to Pierre. I told him about the ashes that said "Die" and the fire at Rom's and of the man in the dove-gray suit who beat me and robbed me of a letter, and finally how I aimed to find that man.

"Why do you want to find him," Pierre asked right off. You could always trust Pierre to have a pertnent question.

"Because people think Crazy James Kincaid did it, and he didn't, and I owe him."

Pierre nodded.

"Because I got a duty to deliver the letters that are given to me," I added.

Pierre nodded again.

"I don't know why else," I said, "cept I feel like I oughta. This man stole a letter to Jenny Smeed, so I figger Jenny's is where I'm going to find him. Not that I know what the hay I'll do when I get there."

I could see Pierre did not like any of this.

"You have bullets for your rifle?" he said.

"Pierre," I said, "I'm not shooting anybody. My business isn't pistols, it's epistles."

"What are you planning to do if you meet this man?" he said. "Write him a letter?"

"I don't know," I said.

"If a grizzly bear came at you," he said, "you wouldn't shoot?"

"Sure I'd shoot," I said, "but I wouldn't hit it. Besides," I added somewhat feebly, "I promised my mother."

He looked my squirrel shooter over. "Take my carbine," he said. "It's better."

"I won't take it," I said.

"Take my carbine," he said.

I took his carbine. But I didn't feel any safer.

When I was packed and ready to mount up again, Pierre did something rare and rich all on his own: he held out his hand for me to shake, which was something he had never once done before. Then when I had shook it, he turned away like he forgot I was there, and I rode off.

It was three days later and late afternoon when I arrived at the Smeeds'. The rain was hissing down in silver needles. The big Canyon lay not half a mile from the Smeed place, and I could have swore I heard its great river, which would be swoll to full from days and days of downpour.

Gabe must have read my fear by the way I slowed him down to a walk. The Smeeds' windows was curtained so you couldn't see in, but lamps was lit inside. I hooked

Gabe wide around the house and edged open the barn door quiet as I could, and got Gabe settled without lighting a lantern. It was still afternoon but you'd a never known it from the dimness of the air. Night felt already upon the earth.

A gun double-cocked in the dark, and I froze.

"Who are you," a voice said by the door. It was Cobb, Mr. Smeed's hand on the ranch. The sound of the rain had hid him coming in.

"Cobb," I said, "it's me. It's Scrib."

When I turned, I saw that Cobb was looking at me hard, and holding a shotgun half raised.

"Scrib?" he said. "What're you doing, sneaking around in here?"

"Couldn't find the lantern," I said.

"It's in the same place as always," he said. "Nothing's changed."

"Been a while since I was here," I said.

"Yeah," he said, "I hear you been busy." I could tell he knew about my trial and all. "You know the Pollacks is dead." He still had not uncocked the shotgun.

"Robert Junior told me," I said.

His eyes noted the gear I was carrying. "A carbine," he said. "That's a change."

"Can't be too careful these days," I said, "what with

people getting killt."

"Ackelberg was out here lookin' for you," he said. "You and Romulus both."

"Yeah, I bet," I said, and tried best as I could to sound calm. "There's been some kinda ruffle. I'll go talk to Ackelberg tomorrow, straighten it all out."

I moved to go out, but he blocked my way.

"Scrib," he said, "I'd hate to hear you fell into bad company. And I'd hate to think you come here to cause anything."

"Hey, Cobb." I tried to laugh that away. "You know me. I'm just a letter writer."

Cobb weighed that, and the shotgun wavered like the tins of Justice as he tried to make up his mind about me.

"Well," he finally said, "come on in."

Cobb followed me cross the yard to the house, keeping well behind all the way. I laughed inwardly at being treated like a dangerous desperado.

We went in through the back door, and there was Jenny Smeed standing at the stove in the kitchen, loading a sheet of cookies onto a platter. When she saw me in the door, her lips made a O of surprise.

"*Scrib*," she said, "where have you been?"

"'Lo, Jenny," I said.

Cobb hung about in the door watching me.

Jenny said, "Cobb, what are you doing lowering around like a cow? Go on, go inside. Take these cookies." She shoved the plate into his fist. "And shut the kitchen door," she said. Cobb slunk out with a warning look at me, but it's hard to make a threatening exit with a plate of cookies in your hand.

Soon as the kitchen door was shut, Jenny said again, "Where have you been, Scrib?"

"Jenny," I said, "that is a whole three-decker story."

"Not hearing a word from Romulus, I wondered and wondered," she said, "what in the world . . . "

"I had a letter," I started.

"You have a letter from Rom?" she said.

"I *had* one," I said. "You might say it went astray."

Jenny's face pinched into a pout and her eyes teared up. "I thought he didn't love me anymore," she said. "I thought he had found someone else. I been fearing for our union, Scrib."

"Rom loves you all right," I said. "He *idyllizes* you, same as ever if not more."

"What did his letter say?"

"I recall it word for word," I said. I was all perpared to recite the message as written, but stopped a second and reflected that all those "forsooths" and "fains" and

155

"most precious mistresses of the moon" was no better than Mr. Spicer's "condiments" and "habiliments" and "foodstuffs," so I recited the letter as Romulus had given it to me.

"He says 'Dear Jenny, I miss you so bad. You are a angel on earth. I can't wait a minute for you to be my bride but I will wait forever or as long as it takes. Signed, Your darling Romulus.'" It was about five times longer in the poetic version and I thought Jenny was going to say, Where's all the moon goddesses, but she said, "Scrib, that is the most beautiful letter he ever wrote. That is *so sweet.*"

"Rom writes a pippin of a letter, all right," I said. "Lean, but pointed. Just like he's built."

She listened to make sure nobody was coming, then pulled me into a chair and lowered her voice. She lowered her eyes, too, and heaved a sigh and wrung her hands as if troubled.

"Scrib," she said, "I—I have another suitor now. Mr. Edward Dexter."

"But you're engaged to Romulus," I said with a sunken feeling. "Don't you love *him*?"

"Oh, I do," she said fervently. "I do love him. But Edward gives me such beautiful things, Scrib. Perfumes and jewelry. You know your self Daddy has not been too happy about Romulus, and is always talking against him."

Poor simple creejulous Jenny, so easily swayed. She come from a good trusting family, and Dexter had tricked both her and her father with his smooth talk and his whiles and his roll of money.

"Edward says Romulus has just been leading me on," Jenny said, more as if she was trying to convince herself than me. "He says Romulus sees other women."

"That's a d——n lie," I said. "Romulus doesn't see anything but his skinny old cattle and pine after you."

"Edward says Rom goes to . . . goes to those loose women in town."

"Another d——n lie!" I cried.

"Scrib, do you remember how I wept when we wrote that last letter to Rom?"

"I do."

"I was weeping because I didn't know what to do anymore. Because like I say," she said with tremolous voice, "I have been fearing for my and Romulus's union."

I was just about to launch into the truth about Mr. Edward Dexter when the kitchen door bust open and Edward Dexter walked in.

"Jennifer," he said, and stopped when he saw me. In one instant our eyes locked and tangled.

"Edward," Jenny said, standing up, "this is my friend

157

Scrib." She went red from the roots of her hair down through her neck and into her boddice.

"Hello there, Scrib," Dexter says, very smooth, as if he had never seen me before. But his eyes was sinister. They said, "Tell her anything and I'll kill you." I noted that one gray cloth-covered button was missing from the middle of his vest.

"What kind of work do you do, Scrib?" Dexter said.

I said, "I'm a manuensis." He had told me to find another perfession, and clearly I had not. That registered in his eyes. I meant it to.

"Edward's from Chicago," Jenny said. "In banking."

"That so," I said. "So you must know that big building, where is it," I said, "at the corner of Arcadia and Pierre. The Tazwell Building."

"I know it well," he said. "But I prefer life out here. Where a man can wear a gun in peace." He shifted his coat tail to show his two loaded holsters. "And protect himself from whatever may come. From young fugitives from justice, for example."

I saw he was about to pull those guns on me and get me arrested when Jenny's father stepped in the door in his undershirt.

"'Lo, Scrib," he said somewhat gravely. "Cobb said you was come."

Cobb showed up in the doorway behind Mr. Smeed. I saw right off that Mr. Smeed did not approve of me as he once had.

"You met our house guest, Mr. Dexter," he said, and clapped a hand on Dexter's shoulder. "Edward's going to be a big landowner in this part of the world."

"He sure will be," I said, "if he keeps killing people for their money."

The room went real still for a second as if everbody wasn't sure they heard what they heard. I had not planned it to happen this way, but it was happening anyhow. Then Mr. Smeed laughed, without any humor.

"What's that you say, Scrib? Come on inside, we're just finishing dinner."

"This man," I said, pointing to Dexter, "this man killt the Pollacks."

I couldn't stop myself now. My chest felt so inflated with fear I could hardly breathe to speak, but words started spilling out of me.

"Was he here the night the Pollacks was killt?" I said. "I bet not. Robert Junior showed me a gray button he found in the room his parents was killt in, and it's the button that's missing right there on this man's vest. I bet this man killt and robbed that rancher up towards Sullivan, too. You ask him where he got all this money he carries around. Ask where he's really from. I made up some building in Chicago, and he said he knew the place. You think I don't know the man who tried to beat me to death? You ask him if he didn't pursue me and try to kill me. Ask him if he didn't put this here." I pointed to a scar by my left eye. "Ask him if he didn't steal a letter from Romulus to Jenny. I bet you'll find that letter mongst his things, all scrawled over with obseenities—along with a barbed whip. And I bet that whip's got some blood on it. Mine and the Pollacks' for starters, plus who knows how many others."

Jenny was a-gape with her hands over her mouth. Her father was regarding Edward Dexter very strange, with glances back and forth to me. You could hear the rain very clear now, pelting on the roof.

Dexter smoothly reached for his pistols, and I would have been dead but a double shotgun click stopped him.

"Don't do that," Cobb said in the doorway. Dexter's hands froze one inch away from his pistol butts and quivered.

"Is it true?" Jenny said. "Is it true, Edward?"

"Not a word," he said.

He had confessed already by reaching for his pistols, so not a word of "Not a word" wrung true.

Mr. Smeed looked a shade lost and said to Cobb and

me, "Well, what do we do now?"

"Take his pistols for one thing," Cobb said, "and tie him up." I could tell by his voice that Cobb had never much liked Dexter, and everthing I said had proved his fears. "Tomorrow I'll get Robert Junior, and we'll sort this out."

"I'm sorry to do this, Edward," Mr. Smeed said, and he quietly took Dexter's pistols away.

"You can't," Jenny said. "You can't tie him up."

"Jenny," her father said.

"I won't let you."

"It ain't a question of let," Bill Smeed said. "We can't let him go, neither."

"Lock him in the cellar," Cobb said. "That'll keep him till morning."

Jenny was grieved, but that's what we settled on. Cobb emptied Dexter's pockets so he could do no mischief, and we walked him outside into the driving rain, Cobb covering him with the shotgun, Bill Smeed close behind with the pistols, and me out front with a lantern. I wrenched the cellar doors open against the wind, and Cobb shoved Dexter down the ladder. By the splash he made when he landed, there must have been two feet of water at the bottom. In the light of the lantern, I made out Dexter's face looking up at me through the storm as I shut the cellar door, and there was nothing but murder on that face. Bill Smeed padlocked the doors. Cobb wanted to hammer a board across to bar them solid, but Bill shouted him into the house over the rain.

"Go on inside, Cobb!" he said. "He won't get out!"

Back in the kitchen we stood dripping and troubled a moment. Cobb said, "I'm sorry, Scrib, if I ever thought anything against you."

"Me too, Scrib," Mr. Smeed said.

"A person can't help their thoughts," I said, and I noted how quiet we were talking. I think we three all knew we had a killer right under our feet. You could feel the danger in the soles of your boots, as if you was riding a boat over shark-enfested waters. Dexter must have looked up in his darkness and heard our steps overhead as we moved into the dining room. Jenny was sitting sunk at the dining room table with her face in her hands.

"I can't believe it," she said. "I won't believe it." She wouldn't even look at us. The remains of a dinner was spread out on the table with a bite still waiting on a fork and steaming coffee half drunk in the cups. That plate of just-made cookies set waiting to be et.

"Now, Jenny," her father started.

"There's no proof," she said.

"There's questions," her father said. "Maybe we'll clear 'em up."

"Questions," she said, "questions," and walked out the room still without looking at us. Her bedroom door slammed. I wondered how thick and tight the floor planks was and if Dexter could hear all this.

"Gonna be a long night," Bill Smeed said. "Who's for more coffee and a shot of something to quiet the nerves?"

Jenny did not return and we three sat amongst the dishes, talking but never raising our voices too loud. I filled them in on all I'd been through while Bill and Cobb siphoned drinks from a bottle of whiskey. From time to time we'd think we heard something outside. Cobb would go make sure the padlock was still fast.

"I never should've let this man in my house, Scrib," Bill said. I noted how he avoided saying Dexter's name. "I think in my heart of hearts I wanted him to steal Jenny away from Rom. I wanted him to make something of her, give her what Rom never could. Rom's never going to have much."

"Romulus loves her," I said. "Jenny is all the riches he wants."

He said, "Lord, what deceits a person don't fall into, for love of his children."

Cobb nodded as if he somehow knew the truth of

that, though he was unmarried and childless himself. The whiskey was making them tired and wandery. And so the evening valleyed into night.

There was a couple things we did not know, sitting at that table. We did not know that Edward Dexter's name was not Dexter but Jefferson, and that he come from Richmond Virginia, and that he had made a whole career out of robbing and killing and seducing for some years before he found his way to the Hill district. One more crooshal thing we did not know was that Jenny was on her knees in her bedroom with her ear to a knot-hole in the floor, listning to that snake whispering to her from the cellar. He was telling her it was all a mistake, he was telling her he was innercent, he was telling her whatever she wanted to hear, begging her to help him get away. What he didn't tell her was, he had a whole arsinal stowed with his horse out in the barn.

The old tallcase clock had just rung three in the morning and we was dozing in our seats when a coupla muffled gunshots sat us up fast. Cobb upended his chair with a bang and Bill Smeed crashed his elbows into the table's dishes.

"What the h——l was that," he said, blinking awake, and the door from the kitchen flew open and Jenny run in, soaking wet.

"Daddy, Daddy," she cried.

We didn't even wait for her to explain, for we already guessed what happened. She had unlocked the cellar door and let Dexter out.

Chapter Seventeen

THE SIEGE

obb grabbed the shotgun and raced to the kitchen door, but the second he touched the knob, two bullets shattered its windows. One shot missed Cobb, one sliced his left ear, and he was on the floor before a third coulda flickt him more serious. We all ducked to the ground and Cobb skittered back on broken window glass in case Dexter come busting down the door. Rain and wind blew in through the shattered panes. Then there was quiet, cept for Jenny crying. Her father didn't even try to console her.

"I'll mind the front," he said, and bending low he slippt out the room.

"Scrib," Cobb whispered to me. "Can you shoot any?"

"I know how," I said. He nodded to Dexter's pistols, still sitting on the kitchen counter where Bill Smeed had left them. Question was, Did Dexter want to get away or did he want to kill us and stop our mouths? Then I thought about those first muffled gunshots we had heard and I bruptly realized what they were. Dexter had shot our horses so we couldn't go anywhere.

A terrible pang stabbed my heart as I realized that my best friend was dead. Gabe had saved my life and now he lay out there alone in the barn, shot in cowardly fashion. The world went empty, and in a rush of anger I grabbed Dexter's pistols. I thought, *If I'm going to shoot at him, I mazewell do it with his own bullets.* I had gone through some further invisible door and I knew something now I had not known a moment before: I knew what it was like to want to kill somebody.

Cobb made a motion for me to patrol the middle of the house. Jenny still sat crumpled in a ruin of tears on the dining room floor. I blew out the lamps in the dining room, but pitch black did not make the house feel any safer. I circled back to the kitchen and found Cobb.

"Any ideas?" I whispered to him in the dark.

"Not a one," he said, "howbout you?"

Lightning flashed the kitchen window, flaring us into view for a second.

"I could try slipping out," I said. "Hotfoot it to the Pollack place."

"You wouldn't see your way in this dark," Cobb said. "We gotta wait till day."

I said, "If I slip out now and lay low somewhere, I can light out when daylight comes. Mazewell do this under cover."

Cobb tested it in his mind for a second. "Okay," he said. "Let's do it."

All my gear was still right there on the kitchen floor, so I grabbed my poncho and my canteen and hooked Dexter's pistols in my belt. Cobb thrust some bread and smoked beef from the larder into my pack for the journey.

I crept into the front room and told Mr. Smeed our scheme. He pressed my arm.

"Good luck, son," he whispered. "God bless."

He now patroled the house with his rifle while Cobb and me stole into a bedroom where a window faced the direction I wanted to head in. All I had to do was slip out, run in a straight line from the window, and get out into the scrub a ways. Come dawn, I could make for the Pollack ranch.

Kneeling beside the bedroom window, I eased up the sash real slow till the window was wide. Rain come blasting in, thrashing the curtains and making things harder. I eased one leg over the sill, then the other, feeling my way slowly, with my heart going so fast I half feared that Dexter would hear it beating out there.

I worked my behind onto the sill and reached my toes down farther trying to touch ground. Just as I touched land, I realized that the housefront was white-washed and I made a perfect target up against it. I kicked off the sill as a gunshot rung out and a bullet slammed into the window frame right where I'd been sitting.

Footsteps come running at me over sloppy ground and I wheeled round to run, but the ground was mud and I slid down onto my hands. My boots slithered around in the slippry mire and I could get no toehold. I couldn't even get a balance to reach for the pistols in my belt, but kept slipping back down to my hands.

A whole nother set of gunshots bruptly rung out from someplace off to my right, and I heard Romulus's voice shouting, *"Run, Scrib! Run!"*

So Rom was out there in the dark someplace. Then him and Dexter must have let loose at each other, for more shots banged out from a couple directions, and now Cobb got into the act and blasted both barrels into the dark from the window right over my head. I doubt anybody knew what they was firing at. Meanwhile I was still slicking around in the mud below the window and could hear Cobb's empty shells hitting the bedroom floor as he reloaded. I hoped he didn't hear me and shoot me by mistake, which is exactly what he was about to do when lightning flashed and lit up the house for a second. In the open field before it, I saw Rom and Dexter standing at a distance, guns out, looking the wrong ways and wheeling round as obscurity fell again and thunder boomed and their guns went off simultaneous at each other in the dark. Cobb's shotgun went off too, and the pellets went *shnk, shnk, shnk* into the mud not too far from me.

"Jesus," I heard Cobb say, and just then I got some traction and peeled off along the house with my hand brushing the side. I knew the smokehouse was straight in front of me fifty yards ahead. I had to look out I didn't run straight into it, so I pushed off the house and veered sideways.

More shots rung out, I don't know whose, because I was running in darkness now, or should I say leaping, jumping every other step so my boots would clear any tussocks of grass that might trip me. If you could have seen me, I would have looked like a person leaping invisible hurtles.

Too bad for me, the storm was down to not much rain and lots of flicker, and when the air flashed again, Dexter saw me and took after me. Then Rom took off after him, and now we all chased each other, lightning flash by lighting flash. Ever time the air flickered lighter, Dexter spotted where I was and changed course to keep after. My canteen was banging against my side and making a racket for him to follow too, so I unslung it as I ran and threw it aside, and threw my pack away to lighten myself. I would have tossed away my head if it had let me run faster.

A couple times I stumbled, and once my foot twisted in a critter hole and I hit the ground and smashed my shoulder, but I summersalted right around and back up to my feet. I did not know which way I was moving—it was enough that I was running some way or other. Then I felt my feet moving up a rise and I realized where I was heading, and even though I had that dove-gray demon behind me, I slithered to a stop.

In the darkness I had run the wrong way.

Lightning flickered and I saw the big Canyon spread out right at my feet, falling off into nothing, the shear edge of the drop not ten feet ahead of me. Then the air shuttered down again, slamming down darkness. I had no place to run. That edge was where I would have to shoot it out. I turned to face my pursuer, and the air flickered the world into view again. I saw him now, fifty yards away and running right at me out of the endless night. I reached for the pistols in my belt.

Then God or geology or whatever you perfer to call it took any choice right out my hands. For as I was reaching for the pistols I felt my self losing my balance somehow, only it wasn't me, it was the rain-soaked earth giving way beneath me. The feeble cliff upon which I stood stood no longer, melting into the Canyon. Then I had nothing a-tall underneath me, and I was falling, slurrying down a long steep muddy slope into the dismal abiss below. Gunshots sang out above me, but all that was far far away, in some other life.

Chapter Eighteen
THE CANYON

I t was a ocotillo plant that saved me. I could have plunged straight to my death in that cascade of mud and wet gravel and stone, but one of those green skeleton hands sticking up out of the rock caught me in its fingers like a slotted spoon and held me till the avalanche died out in the depths below. A lightning flash revealed me hanging on the steep wall of the Canyon like a ant on the side of a giant sinkhole. The Canyon's rim ran in a raggedy line a hunderd yards above me, straight up a grade I had no heart or strenth to climb.

After a time the rain stopped and the air grayed and then blued. The river rose into view, clattering far below.

The light grew to a papery overcast, and I freed my self and worked my way down to a ring of rocks like a small fort not far from the river's edge. I had lost one of Dexter's revolvers in my downward plunge, and when I dug out the other it was so clotted with mud and gravel I tossed the pistol aside. So I hid there and I pondered, but my brain was as overcast as the sky.

You never seen such a lonesome desolation as the Canyon, which is naught but brown rock and red rock and black rock and a murky river. The Canyon made the scrub look like the celestial city. Forlornly I watched a raven swoop down with its claws out and scoop what looked to be a sucker out the river and drop it on a boulder at the verge, where it picked the living fish apart and et it for breakfast. I did not take this for a good omin.

Yet there was other signs. A tiny tree, for a sample, had sprouted in that nest of rocks I couched in and sure enough it was a blue spruce about five inches tall. How a spruce had seeded itself and thrived so far down from its natural heights I had no idea.

Klack.

A noise somewheres. I poked my head cautiously out my fort and scanned my surroundings, but nothing moved cept a early damselfly of a lectric blue who zoomed up and hovered right before my face. I could see ever blue-green band in her tail and her turquoyse eyes and even her little mouth parts working, as if she was speaking or warning me, but so quiet I could not hear her. Then just as sudden as she came, she flitted away.

Klack.

A rock rolled, someplace close. I ducked my head back behind my fortress, and a instant later through a chink I saw Dexter step into view not ten yards away. He was making his way down the margin of the river, stalking real slow on the wobbly rocks with a pistol in his hand and a rifle scabbard on his back. Lucky for me, his gaze was picking through some crannies at the marge. When he turned to scan the slope where I lay, I sat as still as landscape, scarcely breathing and hoping the mud that caked me from my fall would cameraflage me.

Then something clicked like castanets as a family of hairy scorpions poured out the cranny about a inch from my face and raised their tails to strike. I startled backwards.

Dexter fired. The bullet pinged off a stone so close to my head it dusted my hair. I threw up my hands from my hiding place.

"Don't shoot," I called.

"Show yourself," Dexter said. "Very, very slowly."

I rose out my fort, hardly able to stand straight, my legs was trembling in such a palsy.

"Come down here," he said.

With my hands still high, I groped my way over the rocking stones towards him till he motioned me to stop. Dexter grinned under his moustache and showed those rotted teeth. The river ran not ten yards beyond him and looked as heartless as the sea that swallowed my father. I thought to my self, *What a stupid ugly place to die in.* But there's some things you just don't get a choice about. And though my eyes went racing around taking things in and trying to hang onto this world, everthing looked pretty final.

"You won't get anything killing me," I ventured.

"I'll get enough," he said.

"They'll find you," I said.

He shrugged. He didn't care anymore.

"You came between us," he said. "You came between Jenny and me."

"Jenny was never for you," I said. "You were nothing to her. You just give her things and lied to her is all."

He flinched visibly, hearing that. I thought I had no weapons, but I did. He had seduced Jenny with words.

Now my words cut into him like blades. "Jenny loves Romulus Vollmer," I said. "She'll never love you, not if I'm dead *or* alive."

"She loved me," he choked out harshly. That such a creature as Dexter could even speak about love—well, it's a matter to ponder upon at greater length. But now his brows darkened and I saw the murdrous look that he wore in that gully. He cocked his gun and raised the barrel level to my eyes till I was looking down a wide black zero.

"Now you die," he said.

Next instint, the gun went off and flung twirling out of his hand as a arrow pierced his wrist and stuck there like a flag. Dexter stumbled sideways with a groan, and another arrow whizzed athwart him and thwacked into a barrel cactus.

I turned my head long enough to get a glimpse of Pierre high up the slope over us drawing his bowstring and getting a bead down another shaft. I dove for Dexter's pistol that had clattered down a tangle of rocks, but his boot kicked me away. Another arrow lightning-bolted through the space betwixt us and ricocheted into the river.

Dexter grimaced and tore the arrow right out his arm, staggering with the pain.

I had to make it to the river before Dexter got his rifle out the sling on his back. For a eternity I scrambled over the topply rocks to a boulder shelfing the water. The river was creamcoffee brown, so I couldn't tell if it was six inches or six feet deep there, but as I tore off my boots I knew I had to gamble. I leept to dive in as far out as I could when a shot rang out behind me and something tapped me on the shoulder.

The water was frigid as ice melt but lucky for me it was deep. Then when I tried to swim deeper, my right shoulder twanged with pain. I had a bullet in it.

The water right over my head went *tzip*!

Dexter had fired again. Spite of the pain I stroked my arms and kicked my feet to work myself downwards.

Tzip! Tzip!

I expected to touch bottom but didn't, and the current tugged me on like a cold liquid wind. Then the water made a loud commotion somewhere behind me.

Dexter had dove in. When I come up downriver, gulping air, I turned back and seen his head in the water a hunderd feet behind me. Far off up the canyon side, Pierre watched us drift out of his range and scrambled over the slope to catch up with us.

Problem was, Dexter with a shot wrist was a better swimmer than me with a useless shoulder. Stroke as I might, he was gaining fast, yard by yard. A family of cormorants bobbing nearby ignored me entirely and upended for fish, and on the riverbank a bighorned sheep that come down to drink watched me pass indiffrently. Well, the world goes on even when you're busy dying. I figgered if worse came to worst, as it was bound to, I still had my knife in its sheath.

Then a curious sound caught my ear, like a factry going full steam. The top of the water started to bristle and spin into eddies, but got smooth and omnous down the river's middle.

I was headed for a rapid.

Almost as I realized it, I saw whitewater foaming up ahead and a drop-off just beyond it. I kicked and stroked for shore to no avail, getting sucked closer while the roaring grew deafning. Suddenly I was hanging fifty feet over a waterfall with a boiling cauldren at its bottom fringed by razor-sharp rocks. If I got dashed against a boulder I'd get the brains bashed out of me, but if I was sucked into a whirlpool I'd drown and my bones would twirl there forever. Then I pitched over the cataract and dropped like bait into the churning melstrom.

Trapped under water with the wind punched out of me, I swirled in that vilent gray gurgitation, summersalting head over bottom. At one point I bruptly felt my britches get stripped right off me, peeled away by the water like a glove off a hand. Then the surge spit me back to the surface and I was amidst the whirling foam but looking at sky, thrashing and gasping and swallowing water. It took me a moment to realize the rapid was behind me, and I was riding out the last high white waves, facing backwards.

The turmoil not only stripped me of my britches. It also stole my knife. I studied the foaming surface behind me, hoping Dexter had got sucked down and drowned—then his head bobbed up on the stream like a pumpkin. He was not only alive, the rapid had shot him still closer to me.

The sun bust out the clouds just then, and all that bleakness got golded over with a weird majesty. From the middle of the river I could see the lenth and bredth of the Canyon and all its pinnacles and spires and a million shades of color. I was seeing those wonders at a curious junkture of my life, treading water with my assassin just upstream of me. My shoulder ached so bad now I could hardly move my arm.

The water started pulling me fast and I detected the roaring of another rapid not far up ahead. I knew I could never endure a second such battering, so I struck out hard for a slot canyon coming up to my left with a sandbar sticking into the river at its mouth.

My toes scraped sand and I struggled up half-naked through deep soft sludge onto pebbles. I wanted to lay down right there on the shingle, but stumbled forward in my sopping shirt as if I weight a thousand pounds. Looking round I saw that Dexter was heading in to shore too. As I splashed through a stream into the slot canyon, the sun went back out and I begun to shiver vilently.

The slot was all of a beautiful pitted pink rock, and a emerald stream ran through it, but the walls was high and straight and mazed before me in a weavy labrinth that might wind on for miles. The pits in the walls made for plenty of handholds, and I'd have tried climbing but for my shoulder. Twenty yards behind me, Dexter was entering the mouth of the slot. He too was slumped and shuffling as if with some great burden yoked on his back. I spied about for a weapon, but there was not even a stick, for the Canyon was as flat and swept as a dance floor.

How far did the two of us go, with him staggering only a dozen yards behind me, I don't know. But finally I had no force left, and stopped and turned to my enemy, feeling as sorry for my self as if I was somebody else entirely.

The rapid had not taken his rifle. He advanced on me holding it sideways by the barrel like a club. His eyes was fixed on me, but he was exhausted as I was, and when he closed in and swung at my head I easily dodged the blow. He swung again, and I stepped back from it again. He hadn't the strenth enough in him to utter a mortal word. All his strenth was gone into killing.

Swing. Retreat. Swing. Duck. He kept advancing, I kept backing up, and the butt of the rifle went *whoop, whoop, whoop* in the air just before my face like a raven's wings.

I startled as my back scraped up against a wall. He had caged me into a corner tight as a chimney. The rock went off to my left and right in two wings, and I gripped a pit in the wall on either side of me to brace myself as Dexter raised the rifle to cleave my brain asunder.

But what was that sudden thunder rumbling under-foot, and why did I hear the roaring of a rapid when there was only that placid emerald stream? Why did Dexter freeze with his arms raised, holding the club up for the final blow? What was he seeing farther up the slot past the wing of rock? For by the look on his face and the size of his eyes, it was pure hell he was looking at.

It was not hell he saw there, but high waters—the front of a flash flood caused by the rains, a hunderd-foot wall of dirty water that plunged down here from higher up the slot, barreling down like a locomotive and gathering size all the way.

I got saved by the wing of rock Dexter had cornered me in. For in a instant the flood was upon us and Dexter disappeared before my eyes, slammed under that wave of filth as if it was a boulder, while the chimney sheltered me from the blast. Then as the flood bore on through the slot, the backwater raised me and raised me and raised me inside that cranny while I grasped for holds as if the wall of rock was a ladder that was doing the climbing for me. I clung onto grass clumps and the pits in the walls, and the flood had lifted me nearly to the edge when I felt it slacken beneath me and begin to subside. I thought I would be washed back down into the Canyon and lost forever.

A voice rung out right over me.

"Up here, Scrib!"

Not five feet above my head was Romulus, hanging over the top edge of the rock wall with his hand stretched down to me. I grasped his wrist with my good hand, and as the water sank away below me I felt my self lifted up weightless, hauled up through the air, and pulled over the edge of that abiss onto flat dry land.

"I might be lean," Romulus panted, "but I ain't

strenthless." And we embraced each other and cried a little for shear relief on our shoulders.

As for Dexter, I spose some ravens picked him apart for breakfast.

Chapter Nineteen

THE END OF IT ALL
AND SOME BEGINNINGS, TOO

ierre found Romulus and me sitting round a fire as if we was at some weird picnic in the middle a nowhere. For Rom had gathered enough brush for a small blaze to dry and warm me. With a heated knife blade Pierre dug the bullet out my shoulder, and I can tell you that operation sure ain't like it is in the melo-draymas, for I fainted dead away. When my wound was bound, Pierre led us out the Canyon and overland back to the Smeeds. I arrived at their gate still just in my shirt with my manhood bared to the world—overdressed for a Paiute, but scant for society. Well, as my mother might have said, naked I come into the world and naked I returned to it. And washed purly clean, at that.

At the Smeed house there was a good deal of explaination and reunion all round. Jenny wept bitterly at her foolishness and fickleness, Rom refused to hear it and proclaimed her the finest woman since Cleopattera, and Mr. Smeed greeted him as a wise and worthy son. I won't bother to tell you how things got straighted out with the Law, but I will tell you that three Sundays later Mr. Romulus Vollmer and Miss Jennifer Smeed was united in holy matrimoany before the rebuilt hacienda of the Triple X Ranch, with one William Stanley Christmas as best man. When the words "I'd do" was spoken, I flung my hat so high I wonder it ever come down again. Then the eyetinerant Preacher who handled the service looked round at everbody and said, "Well, what in tarnation are we doin' standin' here? Paradise is upon us for a day. *Let's dance!*" And Romulus sought out "Pig Town Fling" on his bran-new fiddle, kicking his heels with Jenny's as he played. Towards dawn I took my sad but satisfied leaf of the happy couple to start on some travels.

I had a new horse given me by Mr. Smeed, a serious-minded creature named Nicodemus, with whom I quickly become fast friends. Nicodemus and I did one final circuit, dropping off the remaining letters in my bag and stopping off to see Pierre at Candle Mesa. Pierre and me sat in honest silents together one last time, then he give me a leather pouch with some pine nuts and the mis-shapen bullet he had wrestled out my shoulder. I wear it still on my belt. The day I posted my last correspondences in Hill and shook hands with Frank the Postmaster, I mounted Nicodemus and started east— first to visit with my mother a while, then to travel farther east to the War and see what part I could take in it. But this great and terrible War is another tale, and I will not write it here. I am sure it will get writ sometime, for my sad addiction to ink continues unabated. It seems a thirst that can't be slaked, seeing the number of pages I have fillt right here.

I will say that half a day out from Hill, just past the triple cactus, I spied a horse up ahead and on his back a rider in a black hat with a bright blue ribbon round it. And having greeted each other joyfully, Tazwell Turner and me faced our horses side by side towards the northeast. The breeze at our backs seemed to urge us onwards and I felt the wind ruffle its way betwixt my hairs, for I had aerated my head upwards for the journey.

We was headed into some various and difficult country, and as we rode we talked of how we longed to cross it and see home. Soon the land begun to rise and ridges wrapped in pines come into view above us, pinions ascending into ponderosas, and way beyond them rose the heights clad in aspens and stately blue spruces. Crazy James Kincaid was hiding somewhere in those regions, camped amongst the penstamen flowers.

"S'long, Duane!" I cried out just for the hay of it, and I hoped he heard me.

Middle of the morning that same day, as we was heading up out the last of the scrub, I spotted a wavy line like a scribble of writing on the white page of the desert. When we come closer, I saw that, out the sand where some ocotillo plants groped upwards like ghosty green fingers, a sweetwater crick bubbled up from nowhere. And we both marveled somewhat at this. And where the stream spread out and run away, there was mallow and grape and horsetail growing at its margin, amidst which we could kneel together and clean our tins till they shone in the sun like golden crowns.

We watered our horses, and they drank gladly.

ABOUT THE AUTHOR

David Ives was born in South Chicago and wrote his first story in the fifth grade, an adventure tale called "The Time Planet," in which three men (one of them very much like David Ives) journey to a planet where all of earth's history takes place in a day. Sister Mary Seraphim asked David to read the story to the fifth-grade class, even though the story made almost no sense, and David has not stopped making up stories since. His stories continue to make little sense, but he never lets that stop him. He has written a number of plays, mostly short and comic, collected under the titles ALL IN THE TIMING, TIME FLIES, and POLISH JOKE AND OTHER PLAYS. He has also written MONSIEUR EEK, about a chimpanzee who washes up in a village named Mac-Oongafoondsen and gets mistaken for a Frenchman, with disastrous comic consequences. The tale makes as much sense as the name MacOongafoondsen but is easier to pronounce. SCRIB is a story he's been wanting to tell for a long time. David Ives lives in New York City these days, with his wife and saddle.